"My kiss *lacked* something?"

His eyes widened. "You think my kiss lacked something?"

A little crease appeared in her forehead as she considered his question. "Well...yes."

He sat up in the chair. "I suppose you've been kissed so many times that you instantly know a good kiss from a bad kiss?"

"No, I haven't been kissed that many times, at all, if it's any of your business," she told him. "But the kiss definitely lacked...passion. Yes, that's it. Passion."

"My kisses have plenty of passion, I'll have you know."

Annie shrugged. "Perhaps you're just out of practice?"

Well, he couldn't argue with that. Still, it irritated him to no end.

"So, you're sorry you kissed me?" she asked.

Josh's attention turned back to Annie as she gazed at him, and instantly he knew he wasn't sorry he'd kissed her. Not sorry at all....

Praise for Judith Stacy's recent works

The Blushing Bride
"...lovable characters that grab your heartstrings...
a fun read all the way."
—*Rendezvous*

The Dreammaker
"...a delightful story of the triumph of love."
—*Rendezvous*

The Heart of a Hero
"Judith Stacy is a fine writer with both polished style
and heartwarming sensitivity."
—Bestselling author Pamela Morsi

THE NANNY
Harlequin Historical #561 May 2001

The Nanny

JUDITH STACY

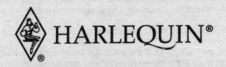

HARLEQUIN®

TORONTO • NEW YORK • LONDON
AMSTERDAM • PARIS • SYDNEY • HAMBURG
STOCKHOLM • ATHENS • TOKYO • MILAN • MADRID
PRAGUE • WARSAW • BUDAPEST • AUCKLAND

Special thanks and acknowledgment are given
to Judith Stacy for her contribution
to the Return to Tyler series.

ISBN 0-373-29161-2

THE NANNY

Please address questions and book requests to:
Harlequin Reader Service
U.S.: 3010 Walden Ave., P.O. Box 1325, Buffalo, NY 14269
Canadian: P.O. Box 609, Fort Erie, Ont. L2A 5X3

To Margaret Marbury, my editor,
for your hard work and support.

To Judy, Stacy and David
for always, always, always being there.

Chapter One

Wisconsin
Summer, 1840

"Mind your own business."

Annie Martin mumbled the words to herself, forcing her attention on the sprouting weeds stretched out in front of her. She was lucky to have this job tending the gardens at the home of the wealthiest man in the settlement. No, more than lucky, Annie reminded herself. Darned lucky. Even if she *was* seeing weeds in her sleep.

Even if she could hardly keep her mind on her own business and her opinions to herself.

The rich earth turned over beneath her hoe as Annie worked her way down the row of tomato plants. Her gloves, trousers and shirt were a little big—better suited for a man. Her wide brimmed straw hat protected her face from the sun. But nothing kept the sound from assaulting her ears.

The baby.

Annie's gaze drifted to the rear of the big white house that belonged to Josh Ingalls, her employer. Windows stood open, letting the gentle breeze cool the interior. Curtains billowed. And the heart-wrenching cries of the baby floated out.

"Mind your own business," Annie mumbled again, turning her back to the house.

She'd worked here only three days, and for the last two she'd heard the baby cry endlessly. It took all Annie's strength to keep from marching up to the house and demanding to know why no one was caring for the child, to keep from pushing her way inside and tending to the little thing herself.

But she didn't dare. She needed this job. Desperately. If she lost it, who in the settlement would hire her? Already people were talking. Annie, her widowed mother and two sisters had moved here only weeks ago; gossip was spreading.

Annie gritted her teeth and turned back to her chore. If Josh Ingalls wanted to run his home this way, allow his baby to cry, it was his business. Certainly not hers. And certainly not her place to criticize.

She stopped suddenly and swept a trickle of sweat from her temple. Maybe Mr. Ingalls didn't know. He spent his days, sunup to sundown—and then some—out in his fields, overseeing the work. At least, that's what she'd heard. Most everyone Annie had met was more than anxious to talk about the elusive Josh Ingalls.

He was handsome, they'd said. Annie couldn't confirm or deny that opinion. She had yet to lay eyes on the man.

Wealthy, they'd also said. From the looks of the fine home, the tended grounds, the orchards, gardens, and hundreds of acres of crops, Annie didn't doubt it.

But the juiciest piece of gossip was about his marital status. A widower, they'd said. His wife dead for months now.

Which meant the handsome, wealthy Josh Ingalls was *available*.

Annie snorted and attacked the weeds with renewed vigor as she imagined all the young, single women in the settlement dressed in their finery, parading in front of him, vying for his attention. While at nineteen years old she was certainly the right age, and could have been just as attractive as any other girl, Annie wasn't interested. She was more comfortable in trousers than fancy dresses, layers of petticoats, corsets and hoops.

With her gloved hand, Annie tucked away a stray lock of her blond hair. She wasn't beautiful. She was tall—too tall for a woman, with not near enough curves, her mother often lamented. But Annie contented herself with knowing that her looks made her passably acceptable. No one gasped and turned away at the sight of her, small dogs didn't bark and children didn't cry out with fright.

Unlike most all the other young women in the settlement, Annie didn't think Josh Ingalls was much of a catch, despite his supposed good looks and wealth. Not considering the passel of children that came with him.

Three, besides the baby. Annie had seen them running wild over the farm. Everyone said they were a handful. Annie believed that rumor without question.

She'd seen the children occasionally. Two girls, ages eight and four, she guessed, with a boy sandwiched between, running through the corn rows, chasing the chickens, always creating mischief. Small wonder Mr. Ingalls couldn't keep a nanny.

All the children needed was a firm hand, Annie decided as she worked. A firm hand and a—

"Mind your own business," she muttered again. "Mind your own business before you—oh!"

Annie grabbed her bottom. Something had stung her on the backside. A wasp? A bee, maybe?

Giggles drifted across the garden. She whirled and saw the three Ingalls children peeking at her through the cornstalks. Peeking, laughing, pointing—and holding a slingshot.

"You shot me!" she exclaimed.

The boy raised the slingshot, taking aim at her again. Anger zipped through Annie. She threw down her hoe, yanked off her gloves and took off after them. The children—completely taken by surprise—squealed and raced away.

They were small and quick, but Annie was mad. She chased them down the rows until they broke free into the meadow. Easily she passed the youngest child, left behind by the older two. Arms and legs churning, Annie pursued them down the hill to the edge of the woods.

She caught them both by the backs of their shirts and yanked them to a stop. The girl screamed. The boy tried to dart away, but Annie scooped him up under her arm and grabbed the girl's wrist.

"Be still!" Annie commanded.

They didn't, of course. A new cry joined their wails. Annie saw the youngest girl standing nearby, unsure of what to do.

"Run, Cassie, run!" the oldest girl shouted. "Run and hide!"

"Come over here!" Annie told her.

"No! Don't!" the boy called, squirming. "Run away! Run fast!"

Annie gave him a shake. "Be still! All of you!"

The children stared up at her, their eyes wide and their mouths open. This, surely, was not the response they'd expected when they'd picked Annie for slingshot target practice. They quieted.

"All right, that's better. Now, come here." Annie led the oldest girl to the shade of the trees. "Sit." When she did, Annie dropped the boy beside her. The youngest girl darted to her brother and sister and squeezed between them.

Annie stood over the three children, catching her breath. All had brown eyes and dark hair, the girls with long braids, the boy with bangs that would need trimming soon. Dirt smudged their faces. The girls' dresses were soiled; the boy's skinny knee showed through a rip in his trousers.

Grimy, disheveled, unkempt. Still, they were beautiful children. It would have been hard to be angry at them if Annie's backside didn't hurt so much.

She bent down and yanked the slingshot from the boy's hand. "What's your name?"

His bottom lip poked out. "Drew."

"This is dangerous," Annie said, shaking the slingshot at him. "It's not a play toy. Why did you shoot me with it?"

He shrugged his little shoulders and looked away. "I don't know."

Annie turned to the oldest girl. "What's your name?"

"Ginny," she told her, looking her straight in the eye. "And we did it because we wanted to. That's why. Because we wanted to."

"Well, you can't do that," Annie declared.

Little Cassie whimpered and snuggled closer to Ginny, ducking her head.

"Don't yell," Ginny told Annie as she looped her arm around her little sister. "Cassie gets scared when people yell."

Annie shoved the slingshot into her back pocket, beginning to feel like a brute towering over the children. Seated quietly on the ground, gazing up at her attentively, they looked like innocent little angels. Annie's anger faded.

"Well, all right, no real harm done, I suppose,"

she said. "But you're not to shoot at any living thing ever again. Not people, animals or birds. Nothing. Do you understand?"

"Yes, ma'am," they chimed together.

"Good. Now—"

Hoofbeats pounded the ground behind her. Seeing the approaching rider, all three children scrambled to their feet. Cassie squealed and climbed straight up Annie's leg into her arms. Annie spun around, pulling Ginny and Drew behind her, her heart racing. She was sure, from the looks on the children's faces, that they were all about to be murdered.

The lone rider pulled his horse to a stop. The stallion tossed its head and pawed the ground.

"What's going on here?" the man demanded.

Annie gulped. Good Lord, the man was huge—tall, with broad shoulders and a big chest. Seated atop the horse, he seemed to tower over them. Brown hair touched his collar. Dark eyes glared at her from beneath the brim of his hat.

"Well?" he demanded again. "What's going on? What are you doing?"

Cassie squeezed Annie's neck tighter. The other two children crowded closer behind her. Annie's own fear turned to anger.

"I might ask you the same," Annie declared, glaring up at him. "What business is it of yours?"

"I know," Cassie whispered in her ear.

The man's frown deepened.

Annie pushed her chin higher. "You've no business charging up like that, frightening the children. Who do you think you are?"

"I know," Cassie said. "He's our papa."

Chapter Two

"He's your...?"

"Papa," Cassie said again.

Annie looked down at Ginny and Drew, who were peeking around her. They nodded.

She dared turn to the man again, withering beneath his harsh gaze. "You're their...father?"

"I am."

"Then that would make you..."

"Josh Ingalls."

"Oh, dear." Josh Ingalls. Her employer.

"What's your name?" Josh demanded.

She gulped. "Annie. Annie Martin. I work here, tending the gardens."

He looked at her long and hard. "I asked you what's going on here."

Cassie buried her face in Annie's neck, holding on tighter. Ginny and Drew squeezed closer.

Certainly the man should know what his children had been up to. Shooting a person with a slingshot deserved punishment of some sort. But with the children cowering around her, Annie simply couldn't bring herself to tell him what they'd done.

"Nothing you need to concern yourself with, Mr. Ingalls," Annie said.

His eyes narrowed. He knew she was lying.

"I objected to their behavior," she said. "I told them so."

Josh's brows went up. "And?"

Annie gazed right back at him. "You needn't worry yourself with the details, Mr. Ingalls. I handled the situation." She dropped Cassie to the ground and urged the children away. "Run along, now."

For an instant they stood there, glancing at their father, then at Annie. She gave Ginny a little push. "It's all right. Go play."

Ginny grabbed her sister's hand and the three of them raced away.

Annie watched them go, feeling the relief she'd seen in their little faces. Feeling, also, the heat of Josh's gaze on her back.

She took a breath and turned to him. He didn't seem to notice her as he watched the children disappear into the corn rows. "Damn...for what I pay a nanny, you'd think I could keep one here."

Josh stared after the children a while longer, then looked down at Annie. "Come up to the house. Now."

He didn't wait for her reply, just touched his heels to the horse's sides and galloped away.

A numb silence hung in his wake. Not even leaves dared to rustle in the trees overhead. Annie stood rooted to the spot, unable to move.

He was going to fire her.

Only a short while ago, everything had—finally—started to look up for her. She had a job she liked. She could help provide for her family.

She could save her little sister.

Annie's stomach twisted into a knot. Of all the things that troubled her, that one was the worst.

Now, like everything else in her future, it was all gone. Simply because she couldn't mind her own business.

Josh Ingalls would fire her. She was sure of it. And why shouldn't he? After the way she'd spoken to him, the way she'd taken it upon herself to discipline his children.

It was none of her business. None at all.

With a heavy sigh, Annie headed toward the house. As she passed the garden, three little faces peeked out through the cornstalks.

"You're gonna get it," Drew predicted grimly.

"Get it good," Ginny agreed solemnly.

Cassie nodded wisely.

Annie drew in a breath, shaking off the fear humming in her veins. "I'm sure your father simply wants to discuss something with me."

The three children shared a skeptical look and shook their heads gravely.

Annie squared her shoulders and marched on toward the house.

"Wait!" Ginny ran after her and tugged her sleeve. "Are you going to tell Papa what we did? With the slingshot?"

Gazing down at the three frightened faces, Annie still couldn't bring herself to tell their papa what they'd done.

"What happened is between us," she told the children. "It's our business. No one else's."

"That means you ain't gonna tell?" Drew asked.

Annie smiled. "That's exactly what it means."

His eyes widened. "Truly? You ain't gonna tell on us?"

"Truly," Annie said.

Instead of a thank-you, or even a smile, Drew stuck out his tongue at her. Ginny grabbed little Cassie's hand and they all ran away.

For a moment, Annie considered running after them. Escape. It certainly seemed preferable to what lay ahead of her at Mr. Ingalls's house.

Annie trudged on. The house came into view. She imagined Josh Ingalls inside at this very moment, telling his foreman to find someone else to tend the gardens.

Her heart skipped a beat as she realized that Josh Ingalls was also looking for a nanny.

Her footsteps slowed as her mind spun. Annie had seen the last nanny leave two days ago. What was it Josh had said in the meadow just now? Something about how much he paid his nanny?

Money. Annie's heart beat faster. She needed

money for her family. If a nanny earned more than a farm worker, maybe she could—

At the rain barrel at the corner of the cookhouse, Annie pushed her straw hat off, letting it dangle against her back, and washed her face and hands. She did her best to brush the dust and dirt from her clothes.

Gracious, she hardly looked fit to enter such a fine home, especially now when she desperately needed to make a good impression. Now, with this great idea bubbling in her mind.

Annie hurried up the back steps. A woman blocked the door—tall, thin, with her dark hair streaked with gray and drawn back in a severe bun. She wore a black dress and a frown.

Mrs. Flanders, surely. Annie had never met the woman, but the other field workers she'd talked to here at the Ingalls farm had spoken of her. She ran the house.

"Miss Martin?" she asked, looking her up and down.

Annie managed a nod, feeling all the more out of place in her plain clothing.

"Follow me," Mrs. Flanders instructed.

Trailing her through the house, Annie found her heart thumping in her chest. Thick carpets with intricate designs lay on the floors. Graceful furniture with carved arms and legs filled the rooms, along with framed paintings, delicate lanterns and figurines. Everything was elegant and pristine.

Except for Annie. She glanced behind her, fearful she'd tracked dirt on the floor.

At the end of a long hallway, Mrs. Flanders motioned for her to stop, stuck her head inside double doors, then turned to Annie once more.

"You may go in," she said, her lips curling downward in a disapproving scowl. "Don't touch anything."

Anger sparked in Annie as the woman disappeared down the hall. Certainly, her clothing was soiled. But that was because she'd been working in the garden, doing the job she was hired to do. And, yes, she was a plain and simple young woman. But that made her no less a good person. Regardless of how the housekeeper looked down on her.

Regardless of what the gossips said.

"Miss Martin?" Josh Ingalls's voice boomed from inside the room.

Annie's shoulders straightened. The man could fire her if he chose. But she wouldn't run away like a whipped dog. She'd have the satisfaction of speaking her mind. And maybe, just maybe, she'd come away with a better job.

Annie stepped into the room. Dark carpets covered the floor. Leather-bound books filled one wall. A moose head with antlers hung above the fireplace. A gigantic desk dominated the center of the room. Josh Ingalls sat behind it.

"Come in," he said impatiently, shuffling papers on the desk.

He'd taken off his hat, and Annie saw that his

hair was thick and dark, the same color as the children's. For once, it seemed, the rumors were true. Josh Ingalls was a handsome man, with a strong jaw, straight nose and clear brown eyes. He looked even bigger seated behind his desk than he had atop his horse.

His white shirt was open at the collar, revealing a slice of deeply tanned skin—like his face—and black, curling chest hair. Even after being in the fields all morning, he looked clean and crisp.

Annie glanced down at her fingernails, then curled her hands behind her.

He made a spinning motion with his hand, urging her closer to his desk as he opened drawers, searching for something.

"When I ask a question, Miss Martin, I expect an answer. A complete answer, not simply what you choose to tell me," Josh said. "So I'll ask one last time. What went on out there with those children?"

"*Your* children, do you mean?" she asked, and stopped in front of his desk.

His gaze came up and he ceased rifling through the drawers. "Yes. My…children."

"I don't know what type of nanny you're used to, Mr. Ingalls, but when I see a situation that needs addressing, I handle it. That's what happened with your children," Annie told him. "If I overstepped my boundaries, I apologize. But I see no need for you to concern yourself further. Surely you have more important matters to attend to."

He blinked at her, taken aback by what she'd said.

Apparently, Josh Ingalls wasn't used to being spoken to in that manner. Annie held her breath.

He shrugged and started going through the drawers again. "That's for damn sure," he muttered. "I've searched the settlement, written to agencies all the way to the East Coast, everything. Why should it be such a monumental task to get and keep a nanny?"

"Perhaps you're not looking in the right place," Annie offered. "Or for the right sort of person."

He glared at her now, clearly not pleased at her criticism. "For your information, Miss Martin, the women I hire as nannies are quite competent."

"Including the last one?"

"Of course."

"The one I saw running from the house two days ago, screaming and tearing at her hair?"

Josh looked away. "She—she took the job for the wrong reason."

"My point exactly," Annie said. "I'm aware of what those reasons are, Mr. Ingalls. You're wealthy. The Ingalls name is to be envied. You, personally, are the talk of the settlement. Women find you attractive and are captivated by the size of your..."

Josh's brows rose. He leaned forward slightly. "The size of my...?"

"House," Annie told him.

A tense, awkward moment passed while they simply looked at each other. A strange warmth pooled inside Annie. Josh seemed to look at her—and really see her—for the first time. Then he swallowed hard and yanked open the bottom drawer.

Annie rushed ahead. "Anyway, unlike all the other young women in the settlement, Mr. Ingalls, I'm only interested in the welfare of your children. That's why I'd make a perfect nanny."

Josh pulled a ledger from the drawer. "Is that so?"

"Yes," she declared, standing straighter.

"You've had experience as a nanny?"

To tell him the truth would end all chances of her getting the job—and the increase in her pay.

"Certainly," Annie said. Surely having two younger sisters and tending an endless number of nieces, nephews and cousins qualified her to look after small children—even the unruly Ingalls children.

He sank further into his chair, studying her at his leisure. Annie felt her skin heat and tried desperately to think of something else to say.

"Tell me about yourself, Miss Martin," Josh said at long last. "You and your family."

A cold chill passed through Annie. Her and her family. Why hadn't she thought ahead enough to realize he'd want this information? Why had she even come in here and asked for the job?

Then it occurred to Annie that if he was asking, that meant he didn't already know. But how could that be? How could he not have heard about her and her family? Was it possible the gossip hadn't spread to the Ingalls farm?

Apparently, it hadn't.

"My mother was widowed several years ago," Annie said, choosing her words carefully. "We moved here a few weeks ago to live with my cousin. My cousin is Angus Martin. He owns the farm that adjoins your property just down the road. Have…have you heard of my family, Mr. Ingalls?"

Josh simply waved his hand, anxious, it seemed, to get on to other matters. No, apparently, he didn't know about her family—or at least, what was being said about them. Annie heaved a quiet sigh of relief.

"I know Angus Martin. Good man," Josh said, as if that were enough. He considered her again. "And you have no interest here but that of the children?"

"Just your children," Annie said. The children and the salary that came with them.

"All right, you're the new nanny."

Annie's eyes widened. Had he just declared her the children's nanny? Had she heard him correctly?

"You start immediately. Go find Mrs. Flanders and tell her I said so." Josh flipped the ledger open, sparing her a glance. "That's all."

She'd come here thinking she was about to be fired, and somehow she'd ended up the nanny—to the worst-behaved children in the settlement.

"If I could ask, Mr. Ingalls, about the wages?"

He scribbled in his ledger, then flipped it around for her to see. "I trust this will be adequate compensation, Miss Martin?"

Annie's knees nearly gave out as she gazed at the

salary he'd written beside her name. More money than she'd ever imagined!

The future opened up to her, full and blessed. Now she could help her mother with expenses. And her youngest sister—she'd make everything happen for her.

All that money, for simply taking care of children. True, Annie didn't know much about children, but it couldn't be very difficult. Even the wild Ingalls brood.

"Provided, of course, that you do a good job," Josh told her.

Annie's enthusiasm cooled a little. "No need to concern yourself, Mr. Ingalls."

"So, we have a deal?"

Annie opened her mouth to agree, but the words wouldn't come out. At that moment, gazing at Josh, something inside her warned her away. It was dangerous here in the Ingalls home…with Josh Ingalls. Not on a physical level. It was something different. Something deeper. Something she couldn't reason out, could only sense.

Josh rubbed his forehead. "Miss Martin, I don't have all day to wait around for your answer."

Would she be a fool to turn down such a generous offer? Or a fool to accept?

Annie didn't know for sure. Thoughts, odd feelings, ricocheted through her. But in the end, her family—her sister—made up her mind.

"Very well, Mr. Ingalls," she said. "I'll accept the position as nanny."

Josh rose from his desk and waved his hand at her vaguely. "Go home and get whatever you need. I'll send a wagon with you for your things."

"My things?"

"Of course. You'll be living here from now on."

"Living here?" A hot surge shot through Annie. *"Here?"*

"Is that a problem?" The tiniest hint of a grin tugged at Josh's lips. "Does the size of my...*house*...frighten you?"

Heat crept up Annie's neck and bloomed in her cheeks. Josh seemed as stunned as she by what he'd said. He turned abruptly and left the room.

Annie sagged against his desk. Leave her home? Her family? Move here? With Josh Ingalls? And all those unruly children?

Good gracious, what had she gotten herself into?

Chapter Three

"You're going to live there? Really? Oh, how exciting!"

"Yes...exciting." Annie managed to put some enthusiasm into her words for the benefit of her younger sister. At age thirteen, Camille still viewed life as an adventure, of sorts, even after all their family had been through these past few years.

Camille perched on the edge of the feather mattress in the small bedroom all three sisters shared in their cousin's house.

"Tell me what it's like," she said. "The Ingalls house, I mean. Is it as beautiful as everyone says? I'll bet there's a library."

Scooping clothes from the bureau and placing them in her trunk, Annie smiled. "Oh, Camille, you should see."

She sprang from the bed. "Could I? Do you think? Could I come over sometime?"

Annie considered it for a moment. As an employee in the Ingalls house, she would be allowed to have a guest occasionally, wouldn't she? She wasn't sure. She'd never worked at this sort of job before, never known anyone who had.

"I don't see why not," Annie finally told her.

"What did Mama say about your job?" Camille asked. "Did you tell her?"

"I tried," Annie said, glancing away.

Camille eased onto the bed again. "She's having another of her bad days."

Bad days for Sophia Martin came more and more frequently as time went on. Annie's mother had never been a strong woman, but she'd held up well enough until their father died. Shortly thereafter, the money he'd left them had run out, forcing them from the home she'd loved so much, leaving them to move from relative to relative, to anyone who would take them in, and Sophia had bounced from good to ill health regularly.

Angus Martin, a widower, their father's cousin, had taken them into his home just weeks ago, after corresponding with Sophia. He'd been agreeable enough with the arrangement—free room and board for the four of them in exchange for cooking, cleaning and running his house while he tended his farm.

All of that had changed the minute they arrived and he got a look at Willa, Sophia's middle daughter. Now he barely spoke to any of them, and Sophia had taken to her bed more and more often.

"You're only taking one dress?" Camille asked.

Annie eyed the blue gingham gown she'd pulled

from the wardrobe cupboard. She only owned three,
and this was her favorite, though she seldom wore
any of them.

"For church on Sunday," Annie said.

"Won't you wear a dress all the time in your new
job?" Camille asked.

Annie glanced down at the clean trousers and shirt
she'd just changed into. Josh Ingalls had hired her
in these clothes, so surely it was all right if she wore
them.

"Here, take all of them, just in case." Camille
pulled the other two from the wardrobe cupboard,
then glanced at those left behind. "You could try to
alter Willa's dresses and take them, too. She won't
be needing them for a while still."

Annie shook her head. Willa's dresses didn't have
enough hem to accommodate Annie's height, but
that wasn't the reason she wouldn't take her sister's
clothes.

"It will just make her cry," Annie said.

"Again," Camille said, not unkindly. "Everything makes her cry."

Annie couldn't blame her sister for crying all the
time. She was pregnant, after all. Pregnant, sixteen
years old and not married.

Willa would have been married, probably, if Evan
Keller's parents hadn't turned up their noses at the
idea of their son being interested in someone with
such limited financial resources. They had bigger
and better things planned for their boy, and had
whisked him away on an extended trip in the East.

Two months later, when Willa realized she was pregnant, there had still been no word from Evan. Shocked and humiliated, Sophia had arranged for them to move here with their cousin Angus, far away from the scandal. They hadn't escaped it, though. The talk had started soon after their arrival. Whispers, at first, then rumors. Angus's attitude hadn't helped anything.

"I'll miss you, Annie," Camille said.

Annie threw her arms around her little sister. She hated leaving her behind, leaving her alone to manage the house, their mother, their sister and their cousin. But, even at so young an age, Camille was a strong girl, with the ability to let most of life's problems roll off her. She found escape in endless hours of reading.

"I have a surprise for you," Annie said, stepping back. "I wasn't going to tell you for a while yet, until I was positive I could manage. But now that I have this new job and I'm making more money, well, I don't see a reason to wait."

Annie dropped to her knees beside the chest in the corner. It contained the few family treasures they hadn't sold off or bartered away. She dug to the bottom and pulled out a pamphlet.

"The Hayden Academy for Young Women," Annie announced. "You'll attend in the fall."

Camille just stared at the pamphlet for a moment, then finally took it, holding it by the edges. "A school? In Richmond?"

Grinning, Annie nodded.

She frowned. "Oh, Annie, it's not one of those schools where all you learn is how to pour tea and curtsy properly, is it?"

"No, silly. It's a real school where they teach mathematics and literature. All the things you're interested in."

Camille shook her head. "But how? We can't afford this."

"I've corresponded with the head mistress and explained our situation. She agreed to let me pay your tuition a little at a time," Annie said. "But since I'm the Ingallses' nanny now, I can pay for it easily."

"Really?" Camille looked longingly at the pamphlet, then at her sister. "Really?"

"Really."

"Oh!" Camille threw her arms around Annie and hugged her hard, then gasped. "I have so much to do to get ready. I'll find the schoolteacher here and see if I can borrow some books. Maybe she can tutor me."

Seeing the excitement on Camille's face pleased Annie no end. Her sister had always been a studious girl, and deserved to go to a good school. But Annie had been motivated to send her by something more.

There was no need for Camille, too, to endure the scandal of Willa's pregnancy. That's why Annie had picked a school in Virginia, far away from Wisconsin. True, there were many good schools closer, but with the great distance, the gossip wouldn't likely follow her.

A little shudder passed through Annie, and she said a quick prayer that Josh wouldn't hear of the scandal himself. Surely, it would jeopardize her job as nanny to his children. And if he fired her, how would she pay Camille's future tuition and school expenses?

"I'd better go," Annie said, aware suddenly of how long she'd taken to pack. A driver and wagon belonging to Josh waited out front for her.

"I'll come by to see you in a few days," Camille said, helping to carry her things through the house, "if that's all right."

"Let me know if there're any problems here," Annie said, though she couldn't imagine there wouldn't be, what with Willa, their mother and cousin the way they were. "Any problems you can't handle, that is."

As the driver loaded her things in the wagon, Annie went to her mother's room, hoping to tell her goodbye. But, as usual, she was sleeping; Annie didn't wake her.

Since Willa spent most of her time walking through the fields, and Angus was working, there was no one but Camille to share a farewell as Annie climbed up on the wagon. They pulled away and she turned on the seat, looking back. Camille, her smile radiant, waved from the porch.

Gradually, the house faded in the distance. Beside Annie sat a strange man. Ahead of her, a new life and—

Josh Ingalls.

She crossed her arms over her middle, the early evening air suddenly feeling cool. Of all the aspects of her new life that awaited her, why had Josh floated into her mind?

And why did those thoughts make her stomach feel so funny?

She shook them away. There was only one reason for her to be at the Ingalls house and that was to take care of the children. They should be on her mind right now, she admonished herself.

Of course, for her to keep her job, Josh would have to be happy with the way she cared for his children. She'd have to please him as well as them.

Annie shook away the thought. Managing four youngsters was no great feat. Goodness, they were only children.

Supper should be served by the time she arrived at the Ingalls house. As the wagon bumped along, Annie imagined sitting in the grand dining room she'd glimpsed today, having supper with Josh and the children.

A family. Dining together, talking, catching up on each other's news, hearing about the day.

Annie's own family had been that way, a long time ago before her father died. Back then, meals together had been warm and comforting.

A little smile pulled at Annie's lips and she found herself looking forward to arriving at the Ingalls home. Her sisters and mother hadn't acted like a real family in a very long time. She liked the idea of being part of one again, even if she was simply the hired help.

What the devil was taking her so long?

Josh peered out the window of his study as evening shadows stretched across the road leading to his farm. There was no sign of the wagon.

No sign of *her*.

Annoyed, Josh turned away, eyeing the ledgers on his desk. He had book work to do and that's what he should be thinking about.

Not her.

He pushed his fingers through his hair. Why was this woman, this Miss Annie Martin, suddenly consuming his thoughts?

Because she was taking the responsibility of those children, Josh decided. Yes, that was it.

As nanny, she was relieving him of a great burden, freeing him to devote himself to things that were important. Leaving him to concentrate on...

How pretty she was. How her blue eyes sparkled. How even in those trousers she wore, her curves were apparent. How she—

"Good God..." Josh turned away, stunned by his own thoughts and his body's reaction to them. Fire flickered in him, unleashing a yearning he hadn't experienced since—

His wife died? Or was it even before that?

The baby was eight months old now. Lydia, eight months dead.

In all the time since that dreadful night, Josh had

had few thoughts of women. He'd thrown himself into his work on the farm, pushing himself harder and harder, guaranteeing that at day's end he fell exhausted into bed and a dreamless sleep.

His life suited him. He didn't want it changed. And he certainly didn't want Annie Martin to be the one who changed it.

She'd insisted she was interested solely in the position of nanny, unlike so many of the women he'd employed in the past eight months. Women who had spent more time pursuing him than caring for the children.

Good. That's what he wanted.

Josh sank into his desk chair once more. When he'd first seen Annie in the meadow today, she'd caught his eye. Then he'd realized she was disciplining the children. She'd offered herself for the position of nanny before he'd had a chance to ask. That's exactly what he'd intended to do when he'd told her to come up to the house.

Josh raked his fingers through his hair, forcing his attention to the ledger open in front of him.

A nanny was what he had. A nanny was all he wanted.

Chapter Four

Mrs. Flanders scowled from the back door when the wagon bearing Annie and her belongings arrived. She directed the driver to take Annie's things upstairs, to wipe his feet, to step carefully, to not dare knock anything over. By the time she turned her attention to Annie, her scowl had somehow deepened.

Mrs. Flanders's lips turned down as she looked Annie over. "Don't you know how to dress? Do you think you're still working in the fields, girl?"

Annie's cheeks flushed and she ran her hands down the rough fabric of her shirt. "Well, no, but—"

"Get on in there and see to those children and their supper." Mrs. Flanders turned on her toes with a huff, leaving Annie standing in the doorway.

She glanced around. No one else was about—no one to tell her anything further, or give any more direction. Certainly no one to welcome her to the Ingalls home. So she struck out on her own.

Annie ventured into the house toward the dining room she'd seen earlier today. Still she saw no one. The only sound was a clock ticking somewhere.

Four children having supper and it was this quiet? Annie smiled to herself. It seemed the Ingalls brood minded their manners while inside; only outdoors did they behave like wild animals.

But when she entered the dining room, Annie saw but one person seated there. Josh.

He sat at the head of the table, eating from blue china, reading a newspaper. The rest of the table, which seated twelve, was empty. A crystal chandelier hung overhead; a sideboard sat against one wall, along with glass cupboards full of delicate china sparkling in the light. There was a fireplace with a beveled mirror above it, and a silver tea service on a cart in the corner.

Josh ate in silence, so absorbed in his reading he didn't notice her standing there.

"Excuse me, Mr. Ingalls?" Annie said.

He jumped. When he saw her, his chest swelled, and she could have sworn his cheeks deepened in color, causing an odd knot to twist in the pit of her stomach.

"Where are the children, Mr. Ingalls?" she asked, surprised that her voice sounded so soft.

He looked at her as if she'd spoken some foreign language. "Children?"

"Yes, sir. The children. *Your* children." She gestured with her hands, encompassing the room. "Have they finished their supper already?"

He gazed at her a while longer, trying, it seemed, to make some sense of her question. Or was it something else? The way he looked at her made her stomach flutter.

Finally, he shook his head, clearing his thoughts. "They don't eat in here."

"Oh." When he said nothing further, Annie asked, "Where do they eat?"

He looked lost again, as if he'd forgotten the question as quickly as she'd asked it. "They, ah, they eat in the cookhouse."

"The cookhouse?"

He shifted in his chair, forcing a frown. "I'm not certain how satisfactory a nanny you'll be, Miss Martin, if you can't even *find* the children."

A wisp of anger twirled through Annie, and she was certain it showed in her face. She forced it away. "Very well."

The cookhouse was attached to the main house by a short, enclosed passageway, which Annie located by following her nose. Delicious smells drew her to the rear of the house and down three steps to the stone walk.

Inside the cookhouse a massive open hearth covered the far wall. A cookstove sat near it along with two worktables, rows of cupboards, and hanging pots and pans. A white-haired woman in an apron—most likely the cook—and two young girls—her assistants, probably—busied themselves chopping vegetables at one of the worktables. They glanced up only briefly when Annie walked in, then went back to their chores.

Near the entrance, the three older Ingalls children sat by themselves at a round table in the corner. Only Cassie ate. As if she were starving, she held her plate to her mouth, raking in the food. Drew sat with his feet tucked under him on his chair, waving his fork around as if it were a bird. Ginny's elbow was firmly planted on the table, her cheek resting on her palm, and she was dragging her spoon listlessly through her potatoes and peas. Annie had no idea where the baby was or who was minding it.

She drew in a breath. Well, this certainly wasn't the picture of family closeness she'd expected.

"Hello, children," she said.

They all looked at her, then at each other.

"What are you doing here?" Drew asked.

"Didn't your father tell you?" Annie asked, annoyed that Josh hadn't informed the children she'd been hired. "I'm your new nanny."

Drew sprang to his knees in the chair. "We don't need no nanny."

"We can take care of ourselves just fine," Ginny informed her.

"Yeah," Drew said. "Go away!"

"Yeah!" Ginny echoed.

"We don't want you here!" Drew said.

"Now, just a minute," Annie said calmly. "I'm sure that if you'll—"

Drew turned his plate over in the center of the table. Cassie screamed.

"Stop that!" Annie reached across the table to grab Drew as he snatched Cassie's plate away. She screamed again. He dumped the food on the table.

"I said stop that!" Annie insisted.

Ginny poured her cup of milk in the mess and started screaming, too. Cassie stood straight up in her chair, stomping her feet, wailing at the top of her lungs.

"I said, don't—" A gob of food hit Annie's cheek. "Stop it! All of you! This instant!"

Drew dived for Cassie's milk. Annie swooped across the table and grabbed it first.

"No!" she shouted, and jerked it out of his grasp.

"What the devil is going on in here?" Josh's voice boomed.

Annie whirled, flinging milk up his shirt and across his face.

Everyone froze. Dead silence fell. Annie gasped and covered her mouth. The children stilled like little stone statues.

Josh just stood there for a moment, milk dripping from his chin, soaking into his shirt, trickling down his trousers. Then calmly—too calmly—he turned to Annie.

"May I speak with you for a moment, Miss Martin?"

Not waiting for an answer, he stomped up the stairs, wiping his face with his shirtsleeve. Annie gulped, wiped the food from her cheek with a napkin and hurried after him, following him through the house and into his study.

"What the hell was that all about?" Josh demanded, flinging his arm in the direction of the cookhouse. "Is that your idea of taking care of those children? I hired you to make sure things like that don't happen. What the devil were you thinking?"

"Stop shouting at me!" Annie clenched her fists at her sides.

His nostrils flared. "I don't need a nanny who will not see to it that—"

"You're right, you don't need me! I suggest you send for Reverend Simon, because you don't need a nanny for those children, Mr. Ingalls. You need a miracle!"

Josh's mouth hung open for a few seconds, then snapped shut. Heat arced from him, coiling deeply inside Annie. He leaned forward. She did the same. Her breathing stopped. Her breasts ached to brush his wide chest. The expression in his eyes deepened, and a peculiar longing covered Annie like a hot, woolen blanket.

She froze. Good gracious, was he going to kiss her?

Good gracious, did she want him to?

Caught in the web they'd somehow spun, they stood like that for a moment, staring into each other's eyes, heat bouncing back and forth between them.

Josh came to his senses first. He turned away suddenly. Annie gulped and backed up a few steps, trying to will her heart to stop its hammering.

"Perhaps..." Josh said, his back to her. He

cleared his throat and tried again. "Perhaps I didn't explain things clearly, Miss Martin. About the children. About how I want things done."

He walked to the bookcase, searched up and down, then pulled a volume from the shelf. "This should clarify things."

Annie took the book, grateful for something to focus on besides him and the beating of her heart. She read the cover aloud. "*How to Raise a Productive Child* by Dr. Solomon Matthews. A book on child rearing?"

"My…wife…sent for it." Josh glanced out the window, as if that somehow gave him strength. He pulled in a big breath, pushing ahead. "The finest minds in the world have laid down exact instructions on how children should be raised. All their wisdom has been carefully committed to this volume."

Annie opened the book and flipped through the pages, scanning several.

She frowned up at him. "You want your children to march about the house? While I keep time by clapping my hands?" It took all her willpower not to add, "Have you lost your mind?"

"What I want, Miss Martin, is *order,*" he told her. "I want discipline. I want calm and quiet in my home."

"But—"

"*That's* what I want. *That's* what I'll have," Josh said. "Or I'll find myself another nanny."

He didn't wait for her answer, just gave her a curt nod and left the room.

Annie watched his big back disappear out the door, heat and energy swirling in his wake.

Order and discipline? The children weren't the only ones in the Ingalls household who needed it.

Chapter Five

By the time Annie returned to the cookhouse, the children were gone, and Mrs. Royce, the cook, was busy cleaning up the mess they'd left.

"I'm truly sorry about this," Annie said, motioning to the table.

The white-haired woman shrugged, as if she'd seen worse. "Not to worry."

Annie found a broom and swept the floor beneath the table while Mrs. Royce wiped everything down. Annie felt the cook's helpers staring at her from across the room. Surely they considered her a failure at her new job already; really, she couldn't blame them.

"Do the children eat all their meals in here?" she asked.

"That they do," Mrs. Royce said wearily.

"Have they always? I mean, before...?"

"Before their mother died, do you mean? Of course." Mrs. Royce shook her head. "That's the way it's done, don't you see?"

"And that was all right with Mr. Ingalls? Even after his wife died?"

"Not my place to ask," Mrs. Royce told her.

Josh didn't want to eat with his children? How odd.

"The children went upstairs," Mrs. Royce said, saving Annie the embarrassment of having to ask where her charges were. She smiled her thanks and took the back stairway to the second floor.

A number of bedrooms opened off the wide, central hallway. The main staircase stood in the middle, and double doors opened at each end of the hall to large balconies on the front and rear of the house. Light spilled into the hallway from a room at the end.

Stepping into the doorway, Annie saw the three Ingalls children dressed in white nightshirts. Ginny and Cassie sat together on one bed, and Drew bounced on his knees on the other.

Three formidable enemies? The thought skittered through Annie's mind. Or three little means to get the money she needed?

Annie took a breath. No. Neither. They were just children. Children whom she wasn't going to let get the best of her. Certainly not on her very first day as their nanny.

"Ready for bed, I see," Annie said briskly, coming inside their room.

The children quieted, sharing glances with each other.

Annie tucked them under their covers. They'd

gotten themselves ready for bed, but hadn't washed. Dirty little feet and hands disappeared under the quilts.

She sighed to herself. Something to work on tomorrow.

"I'll let your father know you're in bed," she said. "He'll be in shortly."

"We didn't do nothing wrong," Drew declared.

"He's coming to tell you good-night, of course," Annie said.

Cassie's eyes rounded as she sprang up. "Papa's coming? He is?"

"No, he's not." Ginny pushed her sister down on the pillow and threw Annie a contemptuous look. "He's not coming, Cassie. Go to sleep."

A little ache throbbed in Annie's chest as Ginny pulled the covers over her sister. Josh didn't see his children at bedtime, or at meals?

Suddenly, she wanted to take all three children in her arms, hold them tightly against her. She wanted to march downstairs and demand to know why Josh paid so little attention to his children.

But it wasn't any of her business. Not really.

Not if she wanted to keep her job.

Ginny gathered Cassie close. Drew stuck out his tongue at Annie and rolled away.

"Well, good night," Annie murmured.

"Hannah," Ginny said, pointing to an open doorway at the rear of the room.

"Hannah?" Annie asked.

Ginny huffed irritably. "The baby."

"Oh. The baby. Yes, of course." Annie blew out the lanterns and backed away.

The adjoining room was small, just big enough for a crib, bureau, washstand and rocker. There Annie found a young woman probably ten years older than herself, rocking a sleeping baby.

"I reckon you're the new one, huh?" she asked, her Southern accent evident, though she spoke barely above a whisper. Her dark hair was pinned up and she wore the same gray dress and white apron as the cooks.

"Yes, I'm the new nanny," Annie said.

The woman hoisted herself out of the chair, cradling the baby against her shoulder. "My name's Georgia."

Annie introduced herself. "Are you the one who looks after Hannah?"

"Doing the best I can since the last nanny left," Georgia said. "That Mrs. Flanders—you met Mrs. Flanders yet?"

"Yes. Briefly."

Georgia rolled her eyes, and Annie got the distinct feeling the two of them shared the same opinion of the woman who ran the Ingalls house.

"Well, that Mrs. Flanders, she don't let me tend to little Hannah here, 'less it's her feeding time. 'Cause, you see, I'm one of the maids and I'm not supposed to do nothing but my own chores." Georgia tossed her head. "According to Mrs. Flanders, that is."

"That's why I heard the baby crying so much?"

Annie asked. "Mrs. Flanders wouldn't let you come in here and take care of her?"

"Yep. Like to broke my heart hearing her cry, I can tell you that. I've gotten right attached to this little thing." Georgia laid the baby in the crib, then lingered for a moment, caressing her wisps of dark hair. "But, seeing as how I need this job, I didn't have much of a choice other than to do like Mrs. Flanders said for me to do, even if it don't set well with me."

Annie nodded. "I can certainly understand that."

Georgia reared back a bit, raising her brows and looking Annie up and down. "So you're truly here just to take care of the children?"

"Of course. Why else?"

Georgia shrugged. "Well, it ain't exactly some kind of a secret, but most of those other women who came here weren't interested in doing nothing more than sniffing around after Mr. Ingalls."

"They hoped to marry him?" Annie asked.

"Not that the man couldn't use the benefit of a little female comfort, if you get my meaning. Especially after that wife of his. Lordy..." Georgia shook her head. "Well, Annie, it's a pleasure to meet you and a pleasure to have you working here."

"Thank you," Annie said, glad to finally hear a kind word from someone in the Ingalls home.

"All I can say to you is good luck. You're a-gonna be needing it." Georgia stepped away from the crib. "I'd better get a-going. You've a room all to yourself, you know, right through that door. I tidied it up for you and unpacked your things. Let me know if you need anything else."

"Thank you, Georgia."

She gave Hannah a little pat on the back, then leaned closer to Annie. "You let me know if you're needing any help with the baby here. Like I said, I've gotten right attached to her."

After Georgia left the room, Annie watched the baby, thankful she was sleeping. She considered checking on the three older children, then changed her mind. They were quiet, and that was good enough. Tonight, at least.

She opened the adjoining door and found her bedroom. Annie fell back against the closed door, staring wide-eyed.

Soft light came from the lanterns beside the canopy bed and on the spacious bureau. There were two chests, a wardrobe, a writing desk and a washstand, all in rich mahogany. The coverlet was pale blue with tiny yellow-and-white flowers. Curtains were pristine white, and a floral rug of rich hues covered the floor.

Heavens, such a lovely bedroom. She'd never even had one of her own before—she'd always shared with her sisters. If she, the nanny, had so fine a room, what must the others be like?

A strange heat swelled inside Annie. Josh's bedroom. What did it look like?

She gasped in the quiet room. Why had she even thought such a thing?

Quickly, she opened the wardrobe and found her

three dresses hanging to one side, her one pair of good shoes resting at the bottom. Her apparel looked meager in the vast cupboard. The rest of her clothing took up only two drawers in the massive bureau.

Though her heart seemed to be beating faster than usual, Annie was tired. She'd have her hands full tomorrow with the children and—

The book. Annie gasped aloud in the silent room. She'd left the book Josh had given her in the study.

What if Josh found it there in the morning? He'd likely think she'd completely disregarded his instructions, blatantly defied him.

Would he fire her? He wasn't all that happy with her already.

She had to retrieve that book.

Annie crept to the door and peeked into the hallway. No one was there; no cracks of light shone from under the other doors. Which room was Josh's? she wondered.

And what was he doing in there? Annie's thoughts meandered for a few seconds. Was he undressing? In bed already?

A little mewl slipped from Annie's lips. She slapped her hand over her mouth. Goodness, such thoughts. She certainly had more pressing things to think about—such as keeping her job.

Annie listened, her ears straining. No sounds. It seemed everyone had retired for the night.

She hurried to the stairway and leaned over the railing. Faint light shone from below. Annie glanced around, then slipped down the steps.

At the landing, she paused, listened and hurried on.

Only the ticking of a clock sounded as she hurried through the house. Holding her breath, she peeked into the study. A lantern burned low on the desk. A book and some papers were spread out.

Josh was still up. He hadn't retired for the evening as she'd thought.

He wasn't at his desk at the moment, but surely he'd be back any second. Annie darted into the study. Where was the book? Where had she left it?

She spied it on a table near the fireplace, grabbed it and dashed to the door, reaching it just as Josh walked in.

He jerked to a stop not two steps away from her, splashing milk from the glass he carried. It spattered his shirt and chin.

He froze, letting the milk drip from his face, and drew in a big breath.

"Am I going to get doused with something *every* time I see you, Miss Martin?"

Annie cringed. "I didn't mean to frighten you."

"I wasn't *frightened,*" he insisted, swiping at his chin with his shirtsleeve. "What the devil are you doing down here?"

Remembering the book, Annie looped her arm behind her, hiding it.

"Well? I asked you a question," Josh said, setting the glass aside and frowning at her.

Instead of cowering, apologizing and begging for her job, as she probably should have, Annie felt her spine stiffen. "Mr. Ingalls, in the future I'll thank you not to speak to me in that manner."

His hand stilled on his shirt. But the outrage she'd seen budding in his expression melted as his gaze dipped, taking in her trousers and shirt, her braid hanging over her shoulder.

Annie's skin burned, even through the fabric of her clothing, as his gaze raked her in a long, hot sweep. Her heart banged in her chest. Heat tingled in her cheeks.

Annie wished desperately she could think of something to say, wished her feet would move so she could run out of the room. But she could only stand there gazing at Josh, who seemed equally paralyzed.

Finally he pulled his gaze from her and looked around the room, wall to ceiling, floor to desk.

Annie lifted her hand to his face. "You have a little drop of milk on your..."

With her thumb, she wiped the droplet from his jaw. But, somehow, she couldn't pull away. His flesh was hot, his beard rough. Heat spread up her hand, through her arm, warming her.

Their gazes met and held for an instant before Josh stepped back. "This is my private study," he said softly. "No one comes in here without good reason."

His words jarred Annie, reminding her why she'd come here in the first place. She knew she looked guilty because Josh's eyes narrowed.

"What's that behind you?" he asked, leaning sideways to see.

Caught dead to rights, she couldn't claim, "nothing," as her instincts screaming at her to do.

Annie pulled the book from behind her. Josh's frown deepened.

"I was reading it, of course," she told him.

He raised one eyebrow. "Of course."

"And I wanted to look up a word in your dictionary," Annie said, waving vaguely in the direction of the bookshelves.

His frown deepened as if he were judging whether or not her claim was believable. Finally, he stepped around her and went to his desk.

"The children are in bed," Annie said. "Do you want to come up and tell them good-night?"

"No," Josh said. He shuffled through the stacks of papers on his desk, not looking at her.

"You don't tuck your children into bed at night?" Annie asked. "Why not?"

He looked up at her. "Because, Miss Martin, that is *your* job."

Annie pondered his response while he continued to sort through his papers. "You don't eat supper with them, or see them at bedtime. Why is that, Mr. Ingalls?"

Josh stopped fumbling with the papers and looked at her as if he didn't understand why she'd ask such an odd thing. "Because that's the way it's done," he explained simply. He turned back to his papers. "Good night, Miss Martin."

He was dismissing her. Sending her on her way, telling her politely to mind her own business, reminding her of her place in his household. Annie wouldn't let it go.

"But don't you miss them?" she asked, taking a step closer.

Josh's gaze came up quickly and landed on her with a force than shook her. Yet his expression wasn't one of anger or irritation at her continued prying. Something else shone in his face.

Maybe it wasn't his children he missed, Annie realized. Maybe it was his wife.

A knot jerked in Annie's stomach. She should have kept her mouth shut. Should have minded her own business. Kept to her place.

He picked up a single sheet of paper, forcing his attention on it. "Good night, Miss Martin."

Still Annie didn't want to leave. She wanted to stay, to do something to make him feel better. The urge overwhelmed her.

But what could she possibly say?

"Good night," she mumbled. At the door she looked back and saw Josh hunched over his desk; from the expression on his face she doubted he saw a single word written on the papers there.

As she climbed the stairs, Annie reminded herself that Josh's feelings for his dead wife were none of her business. Yet, for some reason, her heart ached a little thinking he still grieved for her after all these months.

But what about his feelings for his children? Weren't they her business?

Not if she wanted to keep her job.

At the top of the stairs, Annie peeked into the children's room again. Three little bulges under the covers slept soundly. She checked on the baby, as well, and found Hannah sleeping.

In her room, Annie undressed, washed at the basin, and slipped into her pink nightgown. The cotton fabric seemed coarse, not nearly fancy enough for the room she'd been given. She sat in front of the mirror, unraveled her braid and combed out her hair.

As she climbed into bed, footsteps sounded in the hallway. Annie froze, pulling the quilt over her. Josh. The heavy, measured steps could only be his.

For an instant, Annie thought he stopped outside her door. She shook her head, sure it was her imagination. The footsteps faded and she heard a door down the hallway close softly.

With a sigh she leaned back on her pillows, relaxing on the feather mattress. The book on child rearing rested on her bedside table, and Annie considered reading it. Surely she'd need all the help she could get taming the Ingalls brood.

For her first day as nanny, things hadn't gone so well, Annie was forced to admit. The children had rebelled at the sight of her. A food fight had erupted. She'd forgotten the book her employer had given her, invaded his private sanctum and splashed milk on him—not once but twice.

Annie settled deeper against the pillow, sure tomorrow would be a better day. After all, they were only children.

And tomorrow she'd do a better job of minding her own business. Somehow.

Chapter Six

Dressing like a girl took forever.

Annie lamented her decision as she closed the last fastener on her dress and turned to the mirror.

The green gown—her second favorite—looked nice, she decided, even if climbing into hoops, corset and petticoats took three times as long as dressing in her trousers. She'd coiled her hair atop her head, adding to the ordeal.

But she looked like a nanny, or at least what she guessed a nanny should look like. Mrs. Flanders certainly couldn't peer down her nose at her when she got downstairs this morning.

Annie heard a voice in the room next door and found Georgia tending to little Hannah.

"Slept all night, did she?" Georgia asked as Annie walked in.

"Not a peep out of her."

Georgia lifted Hannah into her arms; the baby yawned and stretched her chubby arms.

"I brought up her bottle for you," Georgia said, nodding toward the table beside the rocker. "Mrs. Royce gets it ready first thing."

"I'll feed Hannah, then wake the other children," Annie said. It seemed a reasonable, organized way to start her day, even if she hadn't read it in a book.

Georgia shook her head. "They're not in their room. I was just there."

Annie was mildly surprised. "Oh. Well, then they're having their breakfast already."

Georgia uttered a short laugh. "I was just down there, and there's not hide nor hair of those children anywhere in this house."

Mild surprise edged toward panic. Her first full day as nanny and Annie didn't even know where the children were.

She resisted the urge to utter a curse. "Could you start feeding Hannah while I check on the others? I don't want to get you into trouble with Mrs. Flanders, but if you could just—"

"Oh, never mind about that Mrs. Flanders." Georgia gave the baby a hug. "Me and little Miss Hannah know a few places to hide out where that cranky ol' woman won't never find us."

"Thank you, Georgia. Thanks so much." Annie hiked up her dress and rattled down the stairway.

"Miss Martin!"

Annie jerked to a stop in the downstairs hallway as Mrs. Flanders barked her name. Hands folded in front of her, the older woman stood in the center of the parlor, glaring at her.

Annie's first instinct was to tell Mrs. Flanders she had no time for her, and to hurry on about her business. But Mrs. Flanders ran the house. Being rude to her wouldn't improve her employment longevity.

"Yes?" Annie asked politely, forcing a smile, feigning interest.

"I want to make it clear to you, Miss Martin, that *you* are to take charge of the children. Georgia is no longer available to assist with them in any way."

Annie pressed her lips together, sure Mrs. Flanders couldn't possibly know that Georgia was taking care of the baby at this very moment.

"A *proper* nanny would know that," Mrs. Flanders told her, indicating by her tone that Annie was just the opposite. Her lips turned down even more sharply. "I understand a girl of your…background…isn't accustomed to living in a fine home such as this."

Annie's cheeks flushed in the face of yet another insult.

"Mrs. Ingalls devoted countless hours to decorating her home." Mrs. Flanders waved her hand about the elegantly furnished parlor. "Do you recognize the workmanship of that cabinet, Miss Martin?"

Annie reined in her impatience to find the children, and eyed the mahogany cabinet with its slender tapering legs, carved feathers and oval, brass drawer handles. "Well…"

"Hepplewhite, the renowned cabinetmaker in London. Many of the tables in this house are Sheraton's, also from London. The wallpaper? Imported from France. The finest crystal, china, silver and linens from Europe.'' Mrs. Flanders drew herself up and looked pointedly at Annie's dress. ''Mrs. Ingalls's clothing was made for her by the finest dressmakers in the East and abroad.''

Annie kept her chin up, fighting the instinct to explain her circumstances and shield her simple dress with her hands. Fighting, too, the instinct she hadn't experienced since she was ten years old—to make a fist and pop Mrs. Flanders in her arrogant nose.

Instead, she plastered on the closest thing to a smile she could manage. ''I'm sure Mrs. Ingalls had exquisite taste. Now, if you'll excuse me?''

''One more thing, Miss Martin. The children aren't to play in the house. You are to confine them to their room upstairs.''

Annie frowned. ''But this is their home.''

Mrs. Flanders raised a haughty brow. ''That's the way it's *done,* Miss Martin.''

''I understand,'' Annie said, though really, she didn't.

She left, forbidding herself to hurry away, but unable to shake off the sting of Mrs. Flanders's words. Had she heard the gossip about Annie's family? Or did the older woman simply not like her?

Either way, Annie intended to show Mrs. Flanders—and everyone else in the Ingalls household—that she was, indeed, worthy of the job entrusted to her.

In the cookhouse, Mrs. Royce and her helpers were busy at the worktables. Steam rose from boiling pots on the cookstove.

There was no sign of the three little Ingalls.

"Did the children have their breakfast already?" Annie asked, trying to sound casual.

The three cooks all looked at each other and rolled their eyes.

"Down early, they were, before I got up," Mrs. Royce muttered. "Fixed themselves a meal of jam and cookies, and a few other things, from the looks of the place."

A vision of the mess the cooks must have walked in on this morning sprang into Annie's mind. She threaded her fingers together. "Do you know where they went?"

"I've no clue," Mrs. Royce said, and seemed relieved that she didn't.

"Well, thank you," Annie said, trying to smile.

It was only her first full day on the job and not only had she lost the children, she discovered they'd invaded the cookhouse and left it in a shambles.

A shudder passed through Annie. What else might the children be up to at this very moment?

Annie hurried out the back door. Shading her eyes against the morning sun, she gazed at the barns and outbuildings, the meadows and fields stretching into the distance. She circled the house twice. No sign of the children.

Sighing, she considered the probability that they would come back home once they got hungry.

Sooner or later, her charges would reappear. She could simply wait them out.

Annie wasn't willing to do that.

Muttering under her breath, she trudged back into the house and up the stairs. Mrs. Flanders might look down her nose at her. The cooks might wonder about her competence. Josh Ingalls could resent her nosy questions.

But those children—those three little children— were not going to get the best of her.

"What the ...?"

Josh pulled his horse to a stop at the edge of the field, squinting his eyes against the sharp rays of the sun. Green rolling hills spread out as far as he could see, dotted by trees and an occasional rabbit and squirrel.

And here, amid this vast emptiness, he saw Annie.

Annie. Josh pressed his lips together as he watched her hiking up the hill toward a spreading elm tree. She had on the same straw hat he'd seen her in yesterday.

And she was wearing those trousers.

Annoying. Yes, annoying, finding her out here, he decided. Yet he wasn't clear on just why he felt that way.

It couldn't possibly be the trousers. Could it?

No. Of course not, he decided, shifting in the saddle. Probably it was because he needed the solitude of his farm this morning. He didn't want to be reminded of problems. He didn't want to make decisions at the moment.

Or was it because he'd found her creeping into his thoughts since daybreak? Without trousers?

Josh snorted, then nudged his stallion's sides and headed toward her.

Good gracious, Annie thought as she saw Josh approach. The man owned hundreds of acres—hundreds. How could he possibly be in the same place as she?

And why had he showed up at this particular moment, on this particular spot when she didn't have the foggiest idea where his children were? Just how was she going to explain that?

Above all, she couldn't let him know that she'd failed so terribly at her new job.

Annie waited as he drew nearer, licking her dry lips, trying to work up some moisture—and a reasonable explanation.

She was hot and thirsty. She hadn't brought any water with her. She'd always lived in towns. She wasn't used to these wide-open spaces. She hadn't thought the morning would turn so warm, or that she'd walk so far, or that she'd get lost. But at least she was more comfortable than she would have been if she hadn't gone back upstairs and changed out of her dress before setting out.

"Good morning." Annie put on a smile when Josh stopped his horse beside her under the shade of the elm.

He leaned on the saddle horn, gazing down at her

from beneath the brim of his hat. "What are you doing way out here?"

"Just taking a walk," she said with a smile and a breezy air, trying to look as if she weren't about to melt into her shoe tops.

"You're a long way from the house." He looked around. "Where are the children?"

Darn. He'd noticed.

"They're here," Annie said, waving her hand, freezing her smile in place.

He raised in the stirrups and looked around once more. "I don't see them."

Annie smacked her dry lips. "Well, we're...we're playing a game. We're playing...hide-and-seek."

"So the children are...hiding?"

"Yes." Annie stretched her mouth into a wider smile. "And let me tell you, Mr. Ingalls, those children of yours are terrific little hiders."

"I guess they are," Josh said, raising his eyebrows, "considering that I just saw them at the pond."

The pond? The children were at the pond?

Annie's knees nearly gave out with relief. Thank goodness. She could go get them and head back home. Still, she couldn't give up the pretense.

"Don't worry. I won't let them know you gave away their hiding place," Annie said. "Well, goodbye."

She'd gone only a few steps when Josh called her name. She turned around.

"The pond is that way," he said, pointing in the opposite direction.

"I know that," she insisted, trying to keep him from realizing that not only hadn't she known where his children were, she didn't know where *she* was. "I was heading for the house."

Josh pushed his hat back on his head. "I don't suppose you used to be a scout with the army?"

"No, of course not. Why?"

"The house is the other way." He pointed again. "Oh."

Josh gazed down at her for a moment, as if by looking hard he could make her confess the truth. Annie was tempted. Tempted to confess all, beg for forgiveness and a ride back to the house. Instead, she glared right back up at him.

He swung down from his horse and looped the reins around a low branch.

"You shouldn't come out here with no water," he said, untying his canteen.

She licked her lips but shook her head. "No, I'm fine. Really."

"Suit yourself." Josh leaned his head back, drinking from the canteen. Little rivulets of water trickled down his chin, his throat and under his shirt.

She watched him as long as she could, then gave in. "Well, maybe I'll have a sip."

Annie accepted the canteen from Josh. Dry as her throat was, she hesitated. Putting her mouth where Josh's mouth had been seemed too personal. Almost scandalous. And Annie had never done a scandalous thing in her entire life.

Finally, good sense won out. Annie tipped up the canteen and drank greedily. The water tasted sweet and fresh.

It tasted like Josh, surely.

"You shouldn't be out on foot like this," Josh said.

"I had no choice. The children were g—that is, they wanted to play a game."

He raised an eyebrow again. "Hide-and-seek?"

Annie could have sworn she saw the corner of his lips turn up, but refused to acknowledge the possibility that she was lying.

"Yes, hide-and-seek."

Annie plopped down in the soft, green grass beneath the tree. A faint breeze stirred the leaves above them and a bird flew over. She gazed out across the fields.

"It's pretty here," she said.

Josh grunted. "You're not much of a farm girl if what you see here is 'pretty.'"

"I've never lived on a farm before, except for these last weeks with my cousin," Annie admitted. "If you don't see 'pretty,' what do you see?"

He walked over and stood beside her. "Money. Money and hard work."

"Money from the crops, I guess?"

"Wheat, mostly. We'll be planting soon."

"At the end of summer?"

"Winter wheat," Josh explained. "It develops its

root system before the onset of cold weather, and becomes dormant. The plants make vigorous growth in the spring before they're harvested in early summer. Winter wheat usually gives greater yield than spring wheat.''

''And, therefore, more money?''

He looked at her. ''Exactly.''

''And plenty of hard work?''

He nodded. ''Always plenty of that.''

''The work seems to suit you.''

Josh looked out over his fields again, then dropped to the ground beside her. ''I love this place. I bought the land with money I'd won from a lucky streak of poker, and started farming.''

Annie wanted to ask him how many acres he owned, but didn't. She didn't want Josh to think she was interested in his wealth, as so many of the other nannies had been.

''My cousin Angus has lived here a while, I understand. He loves the land, too,'' Annie said. ''It's been difficult for my mother to adjust to this place.''

Josh turned to her. ''Why's that?''

Annie stifled a gasp. Why had she mentioned her family? She hadn't meant to. In fact, the very last thing she wanted to discuss with Josh was her family. She was lucky that he didn't already know about them...about the scandal.

''She was worried about moving out here, so far from a large town,'' Annie explained. ''Worried about the Indians.''

Josh shrugged. ''We've had no trouble with Indians in years. After the war with the Sauks back in '32, most of them headed west to Washington. A few stayed behind. One of them is my friend, Night Hawk. Besides, there's a large contingency of soldiers at Fort Tye.''

"My cousin Angus said there was no need to worry," Annie said. "But my mother, well, she worried anyway. It's been difficult for her since my father died."

"They were in love, your mother and father?"

She was a little surprised by his question. "Well, yes, I suppose they were. I mean, they were married for years. Wouldn't they have been in love?"

Josh grunted and turned away.

"Isn't that what marriage is all about?" Annie pushed her straw hat off her head and stretched her legs out in front of her. "When I marry it will be for love. Love and passion. Enough to last two lifetimes."

Josh fell silent for a few moments, so long, in fact, that Annie turned to him. A vacant look had come over his face and she realized how thoughtless her comments were.

"I'm sorry. I shouldn't have said anything about marriage, with your wife gone."

Josh shook his head but still wouldn't look at her. "No, it's all right."

"I won't speak of her again."

Josh turned to her then. "I don't mind. Really. I don't want the children to think they can't talk about their mother."

For a man who seemed determined to spend as little time with his children as possible, Annie was surprised to hear Josh say those things.

"Mrs. Flanders speaks highly of your wife," Annie said.

"Lydia brought Mrs. Flanders with her from Philadelphia when we married."

"Your wife wasn't from here?"

Josh glanced down at his hands. "No," he said softly. "We met when I traveled East on business. Hers was a very fine, well-established family. I was…fortunate…she agreed to the marriage."

Josh sank into his own thoughts, making Annie feel like an intruder. Yet she couldn't take her eyes off of him.

Was this the face of a man still in love with his dead wife? Is that what his expression meant?

A little knot squeezed her chest tight, and for some reason, Annie couldn't bear to sit here beside him another moment.

"I'm heading back," she said, and got to her feet.

He came out of his reverie and rose beside her. "I'll give you a ride."

"Not necessary," Annie insisted. "I'm sure you have more important matters to attend to."

"Believe it or not, Miss Martin, insuring that my children's nanny doesn't succumb to heatstroke is an important matter to me."

Putting it that way made Annie's refusal sound a bit silly. Still, she didn't want to ride with him, didn't want him—or anyone who might see them—

to get the idea she was interested in anything more than his children.

Because she wasn't. Was she?

Annie backed away. "No, really, Mr. Ingalls, I'd rather walk."

He followed as she backed away. "It's too far and too hot."

"No, it isn't. I'll be fine. Really."

Josh stopped a pace in front of her. "Is there some…other reason you don't want to ride with me?"

The breath went out of Annie as Josh gazed down at her. What was it about this man? Sometimes when he looked at her—simply *looked*—he caused the most peculiar reaction.

"Well?" he asked, inching closer.

Annie managed to look up at him. "I—I don't want anyone to get the idea I'm…"

"You're…?"

What was it Georgia had said about the other nannies? "I don't want anyone to think I'm sniffing around after you."

A little grin tugged at his lips. "Sniffing around?"

"Yes," she said, and felt her cheeks grow warm. "That I'm interested in you because of your wealth or…other things. Because I certainly don't—"

He kissed her on the mouth. Looped his arms around her, pulled her close and pressed his lips against hers, blending them together. Stunned, Annie hung in his embrace, unable to stand, unable to breathe. His thighs touched hers. His chest brushed her breasts. And he tasted delightful, like—she had no idea what, for she'd never before tasted anything so fine.

Then he stopped, with his mouth on hers, their bodies still touching. He froze.

Annie opened her eyes. Josh's were already opened.

He released her and she staggered back a step, unsure of what to say or do. Unsure of why the look on his face was so troubled.

Without a word, Josh untied his horse and swung into the saddle. He offered her the left stirrup and held out his hand.

She didn't want to touch him again. She hardly wanted to climb aboard a horse and ride behind him.

But, surely, to kiss a woman, then leave her stranded in the middle of nowhere was considered bad manners.

Annie took his hand and climbed up. The horse shifted and the saddle creaked as she settled behind him.

Josh didn't speak a word during their ride to the house, and neither did she.

What could she possibly say?

Chapter Seven

How odd it seemed, sitting atop a horse in total silence behind a man who'd just kissed her out of the blue.

Odd? No, Annie decided, not odd. Something else. But she wasn't sure what name to give the feelings winding through her. Finally, she decided not to think about it at all.

But the man certainly smelled good. How could she not notice when he sat right under her nose? His hair, brushing his collar, was thick and soft. His shoulders and back were wide, strong. Locked in his arms moments ago, she'd gotten only the vaguest idea of the strength he possessed.

She wondered briefly if she should say something. The silence was awkward. But in the end she decided it best to leave things as they were.

When they finally reached the house, Annie swung down, expecting Josh to turn the horse around and head out to his fields again. Instead, he dropped to the ground, tethered his horse to the post and followed her inside.

Mrs. Flanders made a point of turning as they came through the back door, arching her brows at Annie, as if seeing the two of them together was significant in some way.

Annie cringed. This was just what she wanted to avoid. And she probably looked as guilty as sin—because she was. Could Mrs. Flanders and her probing eyes somehow see that she'd been off in the fields kissing her employer? Would the housekeeper spread that rumor, even if she didn't know it for a fact?

The last thing Annie and her family needed was more gossip spreading through the settlement. Her mother might not survive it. Her cousin Angus would surely kick them out of his home. And sending her sister all the way to Virginia to school wouldn't outdistance the scandal.

But to Annie's relief, Josh disappeared into the house as she went to the cookhouse.

Everything seemed too neat and organized for the children to have come back for their noon meal. Still, she needed to be sure, and asked the cook.

"No sign of them…yet." A note of dread sounded in Mrs. Royce's words. Behind her, the two assistants shook their heads.

Annie got a fresh bottle of milk for the baby and went up to the nursery. Hannah stirred in her crib, just waking from a nap; Georgia was nowhere to be found.

In her own room, Annie stripped off her shirt, washed at the basin, rebraided her hair, then pulled on a fresh shirt. She lifted Hannah out of her crib and changed her diaper.

To Annie's delight, the baby smiled as she carried her down the hall. Such an easy child. Probably used to strangers caring for her all the time.

On the balcony at the rear of the house, Annie settled in one of the rockers with Hannah on her lap.

"We'll keep a lookout," Annie said. "Your brother and sisters will have to come back sooner or later."

The children had lived their entire lives on the farm. They'd roamed the fields, ponds, streams and woodlands freely for years. They probably knew every inch of it, knew it better than some of the hired hands. Small chance they were in danger anywhere, even if they stayed out all day.

While earlier Annie had been determined to hunt them down, now she decided to wait them out.

Annie relaxed as Hannah concentrated her efforts on enjoying her bottle. From this vantage point in the shade, with the cool breeze blowing, Annie could see the barns, outbuildings, orchards and fields. She couldn't help but notice that Josh's horse was still tied out back, couldn't help but wonder what he was doing.

Rocking gently, feeding the baby, Annie let her mind drift. It floated straight to the kiss Josh had given her. Startled, she got out of the chair.

"Enough of that," she murmured to Hannah.

Spreading the blanket she'd brought with her on the floor, she laid the baby down and sat cross-legged at her feet.

"We must figure what to do about the other children," Annie said softly. "That's what's important."

If she was to maintain her employment here, she'd have to do a better job of managing the children. That meant some changes were in order. Annie didn't have to consult the book Josh had given her to know what to do.

Hannah finished her bottle and babbled happily as Annie played with her. Annie couldn't help smiling. "At least one of you Ingalls children likes me."

Gazing out over the farm again, Annie saw no sign of the three oldest. She did see Josh's horse awaiting him. He'd had more than enough time for his meal and should have been gone by now. Why was he still here? What was he doing?

And why was she wondering about him?

What in the world had come over him?

Josh paced back and forth across his study, rubbing his chin and mumbling under his breath. What had he been thinking? Why in the world had he done such a thing?

He'd *kissed* her. He'd kissed Annie.

On the mouth. Their legs had touched. He'd felt the tips of her breasts. He'd wanted to—

"Oh, God..." Josh plopped down in the chair

behind his desk and dragged his cuff across his forehead.

He'd been annoyed with every nanny who'd worked in his home. Those whom the children didn't scare off pursued him like a hound after a rabbit—some subtly, others with blatant propositions. He'd turned them down, each and every one. Josh never believed servants were there for the taking, and he surely didn't want one of them chasing after him.

Yet here he was, kissing the nanny. Kissing Annie. He hadn't kissed anyone since Lydia.

Josh pulled on the tight muscles at the back of his neck. But he'd kissed Annie. Right out there in the field.

He prided himself on his self-control. He was an ambitious man. He knew what he wanted. He got what he went after. And nobody ever got what they went after by running helter-skelter. Making a plan, following it methodically had gotten him the things he wanted in life.

So what the hell had come over him? Why had he acted so impulsively?

Josh didn't know. He didn't even want to think too hard about it. He wanted the entire incident to go away.

And the only way to do that, it seemed, was for him to apologize to Annie.

After an endless string of nannies, she was the first to display even the vaguest ability to corral the children. He didn't want her to quit. Not without a replacement lined up, not with his queries to eastern agencies still unanswered.

Josh paused as an odd little ache tightened his chest. Of course he didn't want Annie to leave, because he needed a nanny. And that's all Annie was, a nanny.

Yes, of course that was all.

Pushing himself out of his chair, Josh left the study. He needed to put this unpleasant business behind him so he could get on with running his farm. He had important matters that required his attention.

When he climbed to the second floor, a melody greeted him. Strange, because the house was usually so quiet. He followed it to the balcony at the rear of the house and found Annie sitting on the floor, her back to him, singing softly to the baby.

A rush of heat spiked in him. The long braid of her golden hair hung down the center of her back. The belt she wore cinched her waist, displaying the natural curve of her hips. Her bottom pressed against the floor.

And he wanted to kiss her again.

No. Josh shook his head. No, he didn't want to kiss her, he wanted to apologize. That's all.

He squared his shoulders and marched out onto the balcony.

"Miss Martin, I want to—"

"Oh..." Annie leaned her head back to look up at him, displaying the white column of her throat, the swell of her breasts against her shirt. "Hello."

She'd been sitting cross-legged on the floor. Now

she put her legs together and twisted them to the side. Josh ripped his gaze from her. "Miss Martin, I want—"

"Sit down, would you?"

He didn't intend to be here that long. "I just want to tell you—"

"Sit down," she said again. "You look like a giant from down here."

Josh grumbled a little, then sat in the rocker beside Annie and the baby.

"I was helping Hannah practice sitting up," Annie said, holding each of the baby's hands as she wobbled back and forth. "She's a bit behind."

Josh frowned and sat forward in the chair. "Are you saying there's something wrong with her? Does she need a doctor?"

"No," Annie said, still focusing on the baby. "She just needs more attention, a little more encouragement. She'll be fine."

He looked at her a while longer, turning his head one way then the other. "She sort of resembles me, don't you think?"

Annie leaned back a little, looking at the baby with a critical eye. "Yes, a little. Hopefully, she'll outgrow it."

"I beg your pardon?"

Annie smiled. "You're a nice enough looking man, but I don't think you'd have made a very pretty woman."

"Oh, well, I suppose not."

"Do you want to hold her?"

"No," he said quickly, and sat back in his chair.

After a few moments, Annie looked up at him. "So, what did you want?"

Those big blue eyes of hers gazed up at him. Josh gulped. A moment passed before he remembered.

"I...I came to apologize," he said. "For kissing you like that."

Annie glanced away, looking thoughtful, then back at him. "You're apologizing because your kiss lacked...?"

"My kiss *lacked* something?" His eyes widened. "You think my kiss lacked something?"

A little crease appeared in her forehead as she considered his question. "Well...yes."

He sat up in the chair. "I suppose you've been kissed so many times that you instantly know a good kiss from a bad kiss?"

"No, I haven't been kissed that many times, at all, if it's any of your business," she told him. "But the kiss definitely lacked—passion. Yes, that's it. Passion."

"My kisses have plenty of passion, I'll have you know."

Annie shrugged. "Perhaps you're just out of practice?"

Well, he couldn't argue with that. Still, it irritated him no end that she'd said such a thing. And after he'd come all the way up here to apologize, to do the right thing by her.

"So, you're sorry you kissed me?"

Josh's attention turned back to Annie as she gazed

at him. Those blue eyes of hers seemed to see straight through him, and instantly he knew he wasn't sorry he'd kissed her. Not sorry at all.

But he couldn't tell Annie that. Especially when he could barely admit it to himself.

Josh pushed himself to his feet. "It shouldn't have happened. Let's leave it at that."

She looked up and gave him the most delightful little smile, which caused his belly to knot. "Thank you for your apology."

"You're welcome," was all he could manage to say before he stalked away.

Annie watched him go, watched his big back disappear down the hallway, his head of thick dark hair descend the stairway. She gathered Hannah in her arms.

"Gracious," she whispered, "that father of yours."

A wail of giggles caught Annie's attention out back. Ginny, Drew and Cassie walked toward the house.

"So they're home at last." Annie got to her feet. "Well, Miss Hannah, seems you and I have a few things to tend to around here."

By the time Annie got to the cookhouse, the children were already inside. Drew had climbed halfway up the cupboard reaching for the cookie jar, Cassie bounced on her toes in anticipation, while Ginny helped herself to a jar of strawberry preserves. The cook and her helpers gave the children a wide berth.

"So, there you are," Annie said.

The two youngest children stilled. Ginny gave her a cursory glance. "You're still here?" she asked.

"Still here." With Hannah in one arm, Annie looped the other around Drew and lifted him down from the cupboard.

"Hey!" he shouted in protest. "We're hungry."

"We want cookies," Cassie said.

"You can have cookies for dessert," Annie said. "But not until you've had a proper meal, and a bath."

Drew struggled harder against Annie. "I'm not taking no bath!"

"Then you'll have no meal," Annie explained. "Mrs. Royce, these children are not to have even a scrap of food until after their baths."

The cook, careful to stay on the opposite side of the room, nodded. "Yes, Miss Annie. If you say so."

"But we're starving!" Cassie cried, tears pooling in her eyes.

"We'll eat from the garden," Ginny declared, heading toward the door. "Come on."

"No, you won't." Annie's voice carried such authority it froze everyone in place, including the cook and her two helpers. She let go of Drew and he scurried over to this sisters.

"There are some new rules around here, starting immediately," Annie said. "You children are not to go anywhere or do anything without permission. Is that understood?"

"But we always go outside when we want," Drew insisted.

"Not anymore," Annie said. "Not without permission."

Cassie's bottom lip trembled. Drew's poked out in a pout. And Ginny's pressed together defiantly.

Annie considered threatening them with something, but she didn't know them well enough to have a clue what would work. So she simply pointed her finger at each of them in tern.

"Remember. No one goes anywhere without permission."

"Fine!" Ginny snapped. The other two nodded.

"Good." Annie drew in a breath. "Let's get baths and have something to eat."

Pleased with herself, Annie set about getting their baths drawn and instructing Mrs. Royce to prepare plates for them.

This wasn't so bad, Annie decided. Just tell the children the rules and that would be that.

What could be simpler? After all, they were only children.

Annie smiled confidently. Ah, yes. Now she had the situation well under control.

Chapter Eight

The children stayed in the house the rest of the day as Annie instructed, but they made it clear they weren't happy about it. They kept to their room, refusing Annie's offer to play a game together or draw pictures. The three of them were quite capable of entertaining themselves, Ginny informed her.

So Annie spent the afternoon on the balcony with Hannah. The baby, unlike the other children, was quite taken with her, which pleased Annie. Twice she saw Cassie peek out of their room, watching the two of them. Once she waved shyly before Ginny pulled her back inside.

They had supper together in the cookhouse, but there was little pleasantness in the meal. At bedtime, Annie tucked the children in and offered to read them a story.

"Could you?" Cassie asked, her eyes bright.

"No," Ginny told her, pulling up the covers. "We don't want a story."

Drew stuck out his tongue at her and Annie left their room. In the hallway, she sighed to herself. The children didn't like her much, but at least she knew where they were and exactly what they were up to. For the moment, that was enough.

With the children tucked into bed and Hannah asleep already, Annie realized she had nothing that required her attention, for the first time all day.

If she were at home with her family, she'd have been busy right up until bedtime. But here, with cooks and maids all under the constantly watchful eye of Mrs. Flanders, Annie had nothing to do.

And suddenly, she missed her family. She'd only been gone a day, but it felt like a year already. Was her mother feeling better? she wondered. Had Willa spent hours wandering the fields and crying, as usual? Had Camille found the schoolmarm and gotten some books to study?

Annie wandered along the hallway, then meandered down the staircase. Vaguely, she wondered where Georgia was. She'd enjoy talking to someone, and so far, the young maid was the only person in the Ingalls household who'd been friendly to her.

Not counting Josh kissing her, of course.

At the foot of the stairs, in the great silent house, among near strangers, Annie paused a moment, feeling lost and lonely. Faint light shone down the hallway from Josh's study, and she followed it, picking her way carefully to keep silent. She didn't want to disturb him. She just wanted—

What? Annie paused outside the study. She didn't

know what she wanted, exactly. But whatever it was, taking a peek at Josh could satisfy it, somehow.

A lantern burned on his desk, casting shadows over his face as he frowned down at the papers spread out in front of him. Whatever he was studying took great concentration, it seemed. His brow was furrowed and his eyes squinted. Once he rubbed his chin.

Did he miss his wife at moments such as this? Annie found herself wondering. Would she have come into his study, rubbed his neck, told him to stop squinting? Would he have put his arms around her? Thanked her for distracting him from his worries? Kissed her?

Josh's shoulders were broad, but they had a great deal of responsibility placed squarely upon them. Care and welfare of the land, the crops, the children, the servants. And from the looks of things, Josh handled it all.

But who watched out for Josh? Annie wondered. Who, now that his wife was gone?

Who, even while she was alive?

His head jerked up and he looked toward her. Annie's first reaction was to jump back into the shadows, but instead she stepped into the room.

"Sorry," she said. "I didn't mean to startle you."

"What's wrong?"

"Nothing," she said, lingering at the door. Annie gestured above her. "The children are all in bed, tucked in for the night, and I was just—" she lifted her shoulders "—wandering."

He looked at her, the lantern light casting his face in shadows, but didn't say anything.

"So, anyway, I'll just…go." Even as she said the words she made no attempt to leave.

He watched her for a moment longer, then said, "You can come in, if you'd like."

"I don't want to disturb you."

"You've already done that."

She grinned. "Yes, I suppose I have."

Annie wandered into the room, her hands clasped behind her, gazing at the fireplace and the moose head above it.

"A friend of yours?" she asked.

"We had a brief encounter."

"Seems you got the best of the situation."

Josh nodded. "I usually do."

Annie's heart stumbled in her chest. There was something intriguing about a man powerful enough to bring down a moose, amass great wealth and get most everything else he went after.

"What are you working on?" Annie asked, wagging her fingers at the papers strewn over his desk.

He glanced down. "I'm thinking of buying a new piece of farm equipment."

Annie ventured closer and leaned her head sideways, studying the illustration. "Is that one of those new combination harvesters?"

Surprised, he looked up at her. "Yes. You know about it?"

"I overheard my cousin Angus talking about it

with some of the other men," Annie said. "But I don't know much about it."

"It's a machine that's designed to harvest and thresh wheat."

"Can I see?" Not waiting for a reply, Annie dragged up a chair to the opposite side of his desk and leaned forward, resting her forearms on the edge. "What does this thing do?"

"In order to harvest the wheat, the grain must be separated from the straw and chaff," Josh explained. "That's done by hand now. The combination harvester will revolutionize the process."

"How does it work?"

"I'm not sure, exactly. Mr. Douglas, the inventor, whom I've been corresponding with, is reluctant to give away too many details in his letters. Afraid I'll build one myself, I suppose."

Annie looked up, studying the expression on his face. "You're not sold on the idea?"

"I have my doubts about how well it will work." Josh tapped his finger against the illustration. "The horse-drawn combination harvester was patented a number of years ago, but never put into wide-scale use. This Douglas fellow wants me to purchase one and prove its worth."

"That's because you have a large farm," Annie stated. "And a lot of money to buy the contraption."

"Exactly," Josh said. "Douglas claims that with his machine I can harvest twenty-five acres of wheat per day. That's almost twice as much as I can do now by hand.''

''Sounds wonderful,'' Annie said. ''If it works.''

''Yes, if it works,'' Josh echoed. ''Otherwise, it's a great deal of money spent on nothing, and a chance that my crop will be ruined.''

Annie sat back in her chair. ''Well, if it were me, I'd want to look this Mr. Douglas square in the eye and get the details from him personally before I made my decision,'' she declared.

''Is that so?''

She gasped softly, realizing that she'd blurted out her opinion when he hadn't asked for it. Still, she didn't back down. ''Well, yes. That's exactly what I'd do.''

Josh nodded. ''And that's exactly what I told him.''

She sat forward. ''It is?''

''Mr. Douglas is coming up from Missouri to explain his machine. I'll make my decision then.''

''Sounds prudent,'' Annie said, somehow knowing that all of Josh's decisions would be. Another moment passed before she asked, ''You're inviting the other farmers in the settlement over to hear the news about this machine, aren't you?''

Josh shrugged, as if he hadn't thought that far ahead. ''Well, yes, I suppose so.''

''When is this Mr. Douglas arriving?''

Josh pawed through the papers on his desk, selected one and held it closer to the lantern. ''In the next week or two, according to his last letter. I don't know for sure. You know how unreliable the mail service is.''

''And things are being prepared?'' Annie asked. She'd seen no signs that the house was being readied for a guest, especially an important one like Mr. Douglas, whose stay would likely stretch into weeks.

Josh frowned. ''What things?''

''Rooms cleaned. Linens washed. Menus decided upon. Provisions laid in. Arrangements for the visiting farmers. And entertainment, of course. You'll have to—''

''This is just one man coming out to discuss business. Not some grand ball.''

''You can't expect a guest to arrive after a long, difficult journey and not have a place to sleep, or food to eat,'' Annie told him.

''I know that—''

''Everyone in the settlement is hungry for news and information. Surely, you'll have a reception for Mr. Douglas so everyone can meet him.''

''A reception?''

''Of course. Or did you intend to tramp through your fields around the clock, then send him on his way?''

''Well, no, but—''

''Then what were you thinking?''

''I was thinking about buying a combination harvester!'' Josh lurched to his feet. ''I sure as hell wasn't thinking about menus and linens and a re-

ception and whatever the hell else you just told me
I have to arrange for.''

With a sweep of his arm, Josh sent papers flying
off of his desk. ''Damn it!'' He stalked out of the
office.

Annie sat frozen in the chair, watching the doorway he'd just disappeared through, thinking—not
for the first time since her arrival at the Ingalls
house—that she should have minded her own business and kept her mouth shut.

She didn't have to get up from her chair to know
where Josh had gone. She only had to hear the slam
of the front door to know he'd left the house.

The need to run after him nearly overcame Annie.
Go to him. Listen to his problems. Help him. Make
things better for him.

But Josh didn't want her help. A little knot tightened in Annie's chest. Why would he? She was the
nanny to his children. The hired help. Nothing more.

Still, for an instant, Annie considered going outside after Josh. The knot in her chest drew tighter
as she thought of him upset, alone, with no one to
talk to.

In the end, Annie decided she'd done quite
enough for one night. She gathered the papers he'd
thrown on the floor and stacked them neatly on his
desk, then climbed the stairs.

Annie stuck her head into the children's room,
then checked on Hannah. All the little Ingallses were
accounted for and sleeping soundly.

In her own room, Annie washed, changed into her

pink night rail, combed out her hair and got into bed.

The second day on the job had not been much better than the first, she decided, pulling the coverlet over her and blowing out the lantern at her bedside.

She'd lost the children first thing, conspired with the maid to deceive the housekeeper, kissed her employer in the field, then pointed out how unprepared he was for guests, and driven him from his own home.

"Lovely…just lovely," Annie murmured in the darkness, settling down on her pillow.

What havoc would she reek on the Ingalls household tomorrow?

At least she didn't have to worry about the children. With her instructions for them not to go anywhere without permission, she wouldn't have to search the farm looking for them.

And Josh, on the other hand, would be gone by first light. She wouldn't have to face him, knowing how she'd upset him.

Those realizations brought Annie a little comfort as she closed her eyes and fell asleep.

The gray of dawn seeped through her windows as she roused the next morning to the sound of Hannah crying. Yawning, Annie dragged herself out of bed, rubbing her eyes, pushing her hair back over her shoulder, stumbling along.

She jerked to a stop at the sight of Josh standing beside the baby's crib.

Chapter Nine

"I didn't do anything to her," Josh said, looking slightly panicked and gesturing to Hannah. "I just walked in. That's all. I walked in and she started crying."

"You could pick her up," Annie told him as she scooped the baby from the crib.

Josh relaxed a little as Hannah quieted, then grew tense when he realized Annie was wearing her night rail. And her hair was down. And she was barefoot.

And he wanted to kiss her again.

Josh turned his head away, not wanting to look at Annie, the intimacy of the situation warming him.

"Sorry," he murmured. "I shouldn't have barged in here like this."

"They're your children. You can see them anytime you like," Annie said, as she disappeared into her own room again.

Josh leaned sideways, peering through her doorway. Then, realizing what he was doing, he straightened again.

"Actually, I came to see you," he called.

A moment later, Annie came into the nursery again, now swathed in a pink wrapper, carrying Hannah against her shoulder.

Lord, how pretty she looked early in the morning. Fresh and rested, soft and natural. No part of her bound for propriety's sake. Josh took a step back.

Annie placed the baby in her crib and changed her diaper. "Did you need something?"

"Oh, God yes—no." Josh straightened, reining in his thoughts. "No, I don't need anything. I came to apologize."

"Again?"

Yes, again. Josh couldn't recall the last time he'd apologized to anyone for anything, and here he was, apologizing to Annie yet another time.

What was it about this woman that caused it? And what was wrong with him that he kept doing things that demanded an apology?

Why had he taken his anger out on her last night? He seldom lost his temper, seldom raised his voice.

And why on earth had he kissed her in the field? He'd never—ever—done such a thing before.

Josh shook his head, clearing his thoughts. He didn't know the answers to any of those questions, and didn't want to know, either. But, somehow, he couldn't tend to the day's business until this matter with Annie was settled.

"So, anyway," Josh said, pushing his fingers through his hair, "I wanted to apologize for getting angry with you last night."

"Well, at least you're not apologizing again for being passionless."

"Excuse me?"

Annie lifted Hannah into her arms. "Your outburst last night certainly didn't lack passion."

This wasn't the response he'd expected, but he couldn't disagree with her. In fact, it pleased him, somehow.

"No, I don't suppose it did," he said, and smiled a little. "Anyway, I'll tell Mrs. Flanders to get started on the preparations for Douglas's visit. She'll know what to do, don't you think? Lydia always took care of these things …before."

The baby began to fuss again. "I'd better feed Hannah before she wakes the other children," Annie said.

"They're already up," Josh said, gesturing toward their bedroom.

Annie frowned and moved to the doorway, peering inside. She pressed her lips together, then spun around and disappeared into her own bedroom. But not before he caught sight of her curves outlined by the morning sunlight.

Josh hesitated a moment, feeling a tug he hadn't experienced in a while.

Finally, he came to his senses and left the room before he had something else to apologize for.

"All right, all right, just another minute," Annie said, in hopes of quieting Hannah as she hurriedly braided her hair. The baby was hungry and needed to be fed, so Annie couldn't blame her for fussing.

But she had to get dressed before she could go down to the cookhouse. Bad enough that she'd already paraded in front of her employer this morning in her night rail and wrapper. She'd been completely befuddled, finding him at the baby's crib. Then, discovering the older children were already up and gone—after she'd specifically told them not to— she'd gotten plain old angry.

But at least her decision of what to wear had been made for her. No dress today. Not if she was going to hunt for the children again.

Annie pulled on her trousers and shirt, gathered Hannah and headed for the cookhouse.

She met Georgia coming up the stairs, carrying a baby bottle.

"Hope you don't mind me butting into your duties," she said, passing the bottle to Annie. "But I heard this little girl a-crying all the way downstairs, and I couldn't just stand around useless as a glass eye at a keyhole."

"Thanks." Annie plugged the bottle into Hannah's mouth and she quieted immediately. "I don't suppose you've seen the other children this morning?"

"Oh, sure. Seen them a little bit ago."

Annie heaved a silent sigh of relief.

"Saw them heading out yonder past the barn," Georgia said.

She tensed. "They left the house? The children left the house?"

"Yep. Just like always. Guess we'll have us another quiet day around here. Well, I'd better get to my duties before that Mrs. Flanders goes into one of her fits," Georgia said, then ambled away.

So, the children had left the house. After she'd specifically told them not to go out without permission. They'd deliberately defied her.

"Gracious," she whispered to Hannah. "What am I going to do with that brother and those sisters of yours?"

Annie went upstairs to the back balcony and sat in the rocker, feeding Hannah her bottle. The morning sun had cleared the horizon now, bringing warmth and light with it. Already workers were busy in the fields, orchards and gardens. Vaguely, Annie wondered if Josh had left the house, too.

When Hannah finished her bottle, Annie took her down to the cookhouse with her, had breakfast and went outside. She made a sweep of the yard, the gardens, the barn and outbuildings, looking for the children. After yesterday, when she'd gotten lost in the fields, Annie didn't want to venture out too far.

Seeing no sign of the children, she went back to the house and staked out her spot on the back balcony. Hannah cooed and jabbered, kicked her feet, rolled around on the blanket, thoroughly enjoying the attention Annie gave her. Finally, around noon, shortly after Hannah had fallen asleep, the children trooped through the field toward the house.

Annie waited until they'd clamored into the confines of the cookhouse before confronting them.

"We did ask permission," Ginny told her, lifting her chin in the air.

"Yeah!" Drew echoed, folding his arms across his chest.

"We asked Mrs. Flanders," Ginny informed her.

"Mrs. Flanders?"

"Yeah!" Drew said.

Annie seethed with anger, yet held her temper. She'd told the children to ask permission before going anywhere, but hadn't specifically pointed out who to ask permission from.

"From now on, I am the only one who can give you children permission to go anywhere," Annie said. "Is that clear?"

Ginny glared up at her. Annie glared right back, feeling a bit silly engaging in a staring contest with a child. But she couldn't let her defiance go unchallenged.

Finally, Ginny jerked her chin away.

"We're hungry," Cassie said. "Can we eat now?"

"Of course," Annie said. "Go wash up."

After she'd overseen their washing and gotten them settled at the table, Annie hunted down Mrs. Flanders.

"You fancy yourself *in charge* of something in this household?" Mrs. Flanders asked, after Annie told her the problem with the children.

"I'm in charge of the children," Annie said, bearing up under the older woman's scowl. "So, please, if they come to you again for permission to do something, kindly send them to me."

Mrs. Flanders drew herself up straighter and looked down her long nose at Annie. "Don't expect me to do your job for you, Miss Martin. If you can't handle the children, I'm sure Mr. Ingalls can find another nanny. He's always looking, you know."

Mrs. Flanders turned away with a huff, leaving Annie with a simmering anger and the same fear she'd wrestled with since taking this job: Josh would fire her.

So many possible reasons to get fired, Annie mused as she headed back to the cookhouse. She couldn't handle the children. Josh might find about her family scandal. She couldn't keep from butting into his business.

Drawing in a fresh breath, Annie renewed her determination to take proper care of the Ingalls children. It was the best way she could think of to keep her job.

Yet taking proper care of the wild Ingalls bunch was harder than she had imagined. That afternoon, they escaped the house again while Annie was tending to Hannah. They also left the corral gate open, allowing the horses to wander away, overturned feed sacks in the barn and came home caked with mud from wading in the creek.

"Take off those shoes," Annie told the children, stopping them in their muddy tracks halfway across the cookhouse.

All three dropped to the floor and pulled off their shoes, Ginny helping Cassie with hers.

Ginny folded her arms in front of her. "Mrs. Flanders says you're not in charge of anything in this house. Not even us."

"Is that so?"

"That's so." Ginny jerked her chin at Annie, and pulled Cassie up from the floor. "Let's go."

The three of them ran out of the cookhouse and up the stairs.

Annie's first thought was to confront Mrs. Flanders again and insist she cooperate in Annie's attempts to manage the children. She didn't, though. Mrs. Flanders had already made her position clear on the subject, and Annie doubted she could do anything to change her mind.

After cleaning up the mud from the cookhouse floor, Annie spent the afternoon upstairs on the balcony with Hannah. It seemed the only way she could ensure the children stayed in their room was to stand guard. Again they refused Annie's suggestion for games, argued about having baths and hardly spoke to her at supper.

By evening, when she'd finally gotten the children into their beds and Hannah asleep in her crib, Annie was tired and frustrated. She stood at the top of the stairs, leaning over the railing, seeing the faint light from Josh's study.

She wanted to go to him. At the end of this long day, with all the troubles she'd endured, walking into his study tonight and seeing him seated at his

desk would seem like heaven. Her chest felt heavy
with the want, the need to see him, to be near him.

For a few moments Annie imagined Josh thinking
the same. Maybe he was lonely, too. Maybe he'd
enjoy a visit, same as she. Aside from his foreman
and field workers, Josh spoke with few people. At
least, as far as Annie knew. Was he in his study
right now, wishing she'd come down and join him?
Wanting some company at the end of the day?

Was he wishing that someone was his wife?

"It's none of your business," Annie murmured
under her breath. She sighed heavily and went to
her room.

When she finally got into bed, loneliness
weighted her down. She missed her mother and sisters. She missed having someone to talk to. Part of
her seemed to be away at her own home right now,
with her own family. Another part seemed to be
downstairs in the study.

"Mind your own business." Annie spoke aloud
in the darkness of her room and pulled the coverlet
over her.

It occurred to her then that tomorrow was Sunday.
Annie fell asleep content with the thought that tomorrow, at least, part of her problem could be rem-
edied.

Annie woke before the children, for a change. All
were sleeping soundly in their bed as she stood over
them for a moment, dressed in her night rail and
wrapper, watching them in the early morning light.

How sweet and innocent they looked, tucked in their beds, breathing softly, their eyes closed. Annie smiled, feeling a little tug toward the three of them.

They'd been through a lot in these last months. Their mother had died. Annie didn't know what sort of mother Lydia Ingalls had been, but surely her loss had an effect on the children.

Then, too, there'd been a parade of nannies through the house. One after another. Some of them—probably most of them—only there to pursue Josh, the care of the children of little concern to them.

And Josh hadn't been a very good father to them. He rarely saw them, barely spoke with them.

Annie folded her arms in front of her, still gazing at the children. What this little family needed was someone to pull them all together. To make them a family again.

Was that a nanny's responsibility? Annie pressed her fingertip to her chin, thinking. Since she really didn't know that much about being a nanny—a proper nanny, anyway—she didn't know the answer to the question. Perhaps if she read Dr. Solomon Matthews's book *How to Raise a Productive Child* she'd find the answer.

Annie dismissed the thought. No, she didn't need a book written by some supposed expert to tell her what to do. She knew, at least, where to start.

"Good morning. Time to rise and shine," Annie called, opening the wooden shutters, letting in the morning sunlight.

The children roused slowly, rubbing their eyes and yawning.

"How come you're waking us up so dang early?" Drew grumbled.

"Because it's Sunday," Annie said, opening their wardrobe and going through their clothing.

"Yeah? So what?" Drew asked.

Annie looked back at him. "We're going to church."

"Church?" he asked.

"Of course."

"Church? Really?" Cassie exclaimed, sitting up in bed. "We can go?"

"We don't go to church," Ginny told Annie. "Not since Mama died."

"Well, today we're going," Annie said.

"Does Papa know?" Ginny asked.

"No," Annie said. "But I'm sure it will be all right with him."

"Papa's going, too?" Cassie asked, her eyes shining brightly in the morning light.

Annie paused. Since she and her family had arrived in the settlement they'd gone to church every Sunday, despite the stares and whispers they got. Yet not once had Annie seen Josh and his family attend services.

But, regardless, Annie wanted to go. The children needed to go. So she was taking them.

"Drew," she said, "run into your father's room and see if he wants to go with us."

"I'm not going in there," Drew told her, drawing back under the covers.

"Ginny—"

"No," she said. "I won't. I won't, and you can't make me."

Annie looked at Cassie, who shook her head so hard her hair whipped around her shoulder.

It annoyed Annie a bit that all three children were too intimidated by, or too afraid of, their father to go into his room and ask him a simple question.

She sighed. Something else to work on.

"Fine," Annie declared. "I'll ask him myself."

All three children gazed up at her with their eyes wide and their mouths open.

"Get yourselves washed. I'll be back in a few minutes to pick out your clothes," Annie said to the children. "We'll leave shortly."

Determinedly, she walked out of their bedroom and down the hall to Josh's room. Her feet dragged to a stop.

The door was closed tight. Annie leaned closer, listening. No sound reached her ears.

She knocked gently. There was no answer. She knocked again. Still no response.

Perhaps Josh was up already, up and gone. Was she knocking on the door to an empty room, wasting time? She certainly didn't want to arrive late for church. Arriving late meant everyone turned and stared. Seeing her, knowing the family scandal that was brewing, they'd surely point and whisper.

And that might lead to Josh asking questions.

Annie was certainly having none of that. She glanced up and down the hallway, saw no one, then drew in a deep breath.

She turned the doorknob and peered into Josh's bedroom.

Chapter Ten

Golden morning light filtered through the partially closed shutters, leaving the room in semidarkness. Annie eased the door to Josh's bedroom open a few inches.

There was no snoring, no heavy breathing, no one shouting at her to close the door and go away, which led her to believe maybe Josh was already up.

The room was large, she realized, much larger than her own. From where she stood, a bureau, writing desk and upholstered chair came into view. She swung the door open wider and saw the bed in the center of the room.

It was a massive four-poster made of mahogany, heavy and masculine, like the other pieces of furniture. The coverlet was dark blue. It skittered through Annie's mind that Josh must have redone the room after his wife's death; nothing there hinted of femininity.

Annie ventured farther into the room. A tangle of

covers and pillows was heaped in the center of the bed. She stopped still in her tracks.

Josh.

In bed.

At least, she thought it was Josh. She couldn't be sure. The only thing visible was a long, broad back and arms spread out to the sides.

He lay sprawled on his belly, head buried beneath a half-dozen pillows, the sheet—thank goodness— draped over his hips. One leg stuck out the bottom.

Annie's breath left her in a single wheeze. Odd little tremors caused her knees to shake. She'd never seen a man in bed before, at least not a man like Josh.

There were muscles everywhere. Hard and corded. Powerful, even in sleep. Flesh, smooth and sprinkled with fine hair, browned by the sun.

Annie had never imagined a man's body could be beautiful. But it was. Josh's was.

And never—ever—had Annie wanted to touch a man's body before. But now she did. Josh's body.

No wonder all the women in the settlement pursued him. Obviously, it wasn't just for his money.

Annie slapped her palm against her forehead. Good gracious, what was she thinking? And doing? Ogling a naked man while he slept.

Her stomach rolled. Naked? Was Josh naked beneath that thin sheet?

Her breath came in short little puffs as Annie considered making a break for the door and forgetting the whole idea of disturbing him and of going to services.

But now, more than ever, she needed to go to church, especially after the thoughts she'd just been having.

Annie straightened her shoulders and approached the bed.

"Mr. Ingalls?" she called softly.

He didn't move.

"Mr. Ingalls?" she said, a little louder.

Still, no response.

Gracious, the man slept like the dead. No wonder he hadn't heard her knock on the door.

Now Annie was a bit annoyed. She'd come in here to do the right thing—ask the man if he wanted to go to church with his own children—and here she was in this compromising position. What if one of the servants came along and discovered her in here? What if Mrs. Flanders found her? Annie cringed at the thought of the gossip that would surely follow.

She was certainly having none of that.

"Mr. Ingalls?" Annie called, putting more force into her voice. When Josh still didn't move, Annie shouted, "Mr. Ingalls!"

In a flurry of arms, legs, sheets and flying pillows, Josh sat up, hair sticking out, eyes wide.

"What!"

Annie gasped as he grabbed the sheet at the last second and pulled it over his lap.

"What's wrong? What happened?" he demanded, looking wild-eyed and disoriented. He squinted at Annie, recognizing her at last, then glared at her and pulled the sheet a little higher. "What the devil are you doing sneaking into my room?"

Like quicksilver, Annie's embarrassment turned to anger. "I'm certainly not here because of you, if that's what you're thinking."

His eyes widened. "You're *not?*"

"No, I most certainly am not," Annie told him and tossed her head. "My, but you certainly have a high opinion of yourself."

"Well, you're *here,* aren't you?" he asked, sweeping his arm around the room.

"Just because you fancied that all the other nannies were pursuing you, don't for a minute think that I'm like them."

"And what else am I supposed to think?" he demanded.

Annie propped her hands on her hips. "I came to ask you a question. And, Mr. Ingalls, if you had a decent relationship with your children, one of them could have come in here instead of me."

"You're saying this is *my* fault?"

She put her nose in the air. "Obviously."

"Lord…" Josh pushed his fingers through his hair and sighed heavily. A moment passed while he just looked at her. "All right, Miss Martin, I give up. What do you want?"

Annie shifted uncomfortably, glad she had a good reason for being here. "It's Sunday. Church services will start soon and—"

A string of mumbled curses slipped from Josh's lips. "Sunday is my only day to rest. I don't want to go—"

"I don't care if you want to go or not," Annie told him. "Stay home, if that's what suits you. But the children and I are going."

He raised an eyebrow at her. "You're taking the children?"

"Of course," Annie said. "I'll need to use one of your wagons and a team, though."

Another moment passed while Josh stared at her. "Do you know how to drive a team, Miss Martin?"

"Well, no, I've never actually driven one before," Annie admitted. "But how hard can it be? I've seen it done hundreds of times. Just flick the reins and off we go."

Josh dragged both hands down his face, then braced them on the bed behind him.

"It doesn't work that way," he said, with more patience than she'd expected.

"Then I'll ask one of the field workers to drive us," Annie said, waving her hand, dismissing his concern. "But we're going. The children need an outing and I...I want to see my family. So we're going."

Josh mumbled under his breath again, then uttered a heavy, resigned sigh. "All right. I'll take you."

"No."

His expression soured. "No?"

"No," Annie told him. "I want to enjoy the day,

and I don't want you there if you're going to be disagreeable and grumpy the whole time.''

His shoulders straightened. ''Is that so?'' he challenged.

''Yes,'' Annie said, glaring right back at him. ''That's so.''

They eyed each other for a long moment, an odd tension between them that Annie couldn't ignore. She'd felt it before with Josh. Only with Josh.

''No promises, Miss Martin,'' he said, reaching for the sheet. ''Except that you're going to get quite a show if you don't leave my room right now.''

She supposed he expected her to squeal and run away. Instead, she waited a fraction of a second, then turned and left the room with her head high, displaying what she hoped was regal aplomb.

When his door closed with a thud, Josh fell back on the bed. Damn, what a sight to wake to. A woman in his room. He'd had no female in there since three nannies ago, when he'd fallen into bed one night and found Miss What's-her-name there waiting for him; he'd sent her on her way that very night.

Josh rolled over and looped his arm around a pillow. Somehow, his whole room smelled like Annie now. She'd only been in there for a few minutes, but still...

There was something about Annie. She wasn't like the other nannies, or the other women in the settlement. For some reason, she kept creeping into his thoughts, even into his dreams—

Josh sat upright in the bed, remembering the dream he'd had just before Annie awakened him. He rubbed his eyes, seeing again the eagle sweeping through the sky. His old friend Night Hawk had been there, too. Both of them were trying to tell him something. But, as so often happened with dreams, Josh hadn't been able to hear the words or understand what they were saying. Something important, he was sure of that. But what?

Rolling out of bed, Josh went to the window and looked out. His friend had a wife and a new baby now. He hadn't seen Night Hawk in a while.

Josh turned away from the window. He hadn't *wanted* to see his old friend in a while. He thought about going to Night Hawk's cabin out by the lake, but disregarded the notion.

He had to go to church. He couldn't let his children loose in a wagon driven by a woman who thought "flicking the reins" would get them there unharmed.

Without wanting to, Josh let Annie come into his mind again, and somehow he knew that if anyone could accomplish such a task, it would be her.

Annie's knees shook as she crossed the hall, heading from Josh's bedroom toward her own room, then nearly gave out completely when she saw one of the servants standing at the top of the stairs, watching her.

"Morning to you," Georgia called. "Brought Miss Hannah her bottle."

"I—I was just asking Mr. Ingalls if he wanted to go to church with us this morning," she rushed to explain.

Georgia shrugged. "I 'spect that's the most that's gone on in that room of his in quite some time."

"We were just talking," Annie said, not sure why she sounded so guilty when, in fact, she wasn't.

"I'll start Hannah on her bottle," Georgia said, and disappeared into the children's room.

Annie hesitated a moment. She was tempted to go to Georgia and explain again that nothing untoward had gone on with Josh. But, finally, she decided that making too much of it might make her look more guilty. Besides, Georgia didn't seem to be stunned by seeing Annie leaving Josh's room; she doubted she was the type to spread gossip.

Annie went into her room and dressed in her favorite blue dress, along with the required corset, petticoats and hoops, and swept her hair atop her head. She gave herself only a cursory glance in the mirror before going into Hannah's room.

Georgia sat in the rocker, feeding the baby. She seemed to sense Annie's discomfort.

"Don't go to thinking I believe you and the mister were up to something in his room just now," Georgia said. "Lord knows that man has run off more than enough women in this settlement to make his feelings known on the subject."

Annie relaxed a little. "I guess he misses his wife so much he's not interested in another woman."

"I've got my doubts about that," Georgia declared, rolling her eyes.

"What do you mean?" Annie asked.

"That wife of his. She was one prim and proper lady." Georgia shook her head. "Damn waste, if you ask me. A man like him? Lord have mercy."

A flash of heat shook Annie. She darted into the children's room.

To her surprise, she found all three of the children already dressed in their Sunday clothing.

"My goodness, how nice you all look," she praised. "Did you pick out the clothes, Ginny?"

The older girl glanced up from braiding Cassie's hair and uttered a short, "Yes."

"Very well done," she said. "Now, let's go down for breakfast."

Annie loaded the baby's needs into a drawstring bag, then took Hannah from Georgia and went down to the cookhouse with the children. Mrs. Royce got their meal on the table quickly and they sat down.

Cassie squirmed in her chair, for once hardly eating. Finally, she looked up at Annie. "Is Papa going to church with us?"

The other two children stopped eating and turned to Annie, waiting for her reply. She wasn't sure if they were anxious for Josh to join them, or afraid that he would.

"Your father is going to church." Annie shifted Hannah higher on her shoulder. "Is that all right?"

The children looked at each other, then turned back to their food, not saying anything.

Once they'd finished eating and had washed up, they headed out front. Annie had expected a wagon, similar to the one that had brought her and her belongings to the Ingalls home that first day to be waiting. Instead, a two-seated surrey with a flat roof stood at the foot of the steps. Josh busied himself checking the horses' harness.

He turned when he heard them on the porch. Like the other men in the settlement, Josh didn't wear a cravat and coat to services. His pale blue shirt looked crisp. He wore a different hat, this one black, not the slightly battered one he wore while he worked.

As Annie drew nearer with the children, she saw that his hair was still damp. His face, freshly shaved, was smooth, soft. He smelled of soap.

"Something not to your liking, Miss Martin?" Josh asked, catching her staring at him.

Her cheeks flushed and she ignored his question.

"Ginny and Drew will sit up front," Annie declared. "Cassie, you sit in the back with Hannah and me."

Josh lifted all three children into the surrey as Annie had directed, then reached for her. Instead, she thrust Hannah at him.

He grunted and shifted awkwardly, getting a hold on the baby, giving Annie a hard look in the process.

"She won't bite," Annie told him, then grinned. "No teeth."

Josh frowned down at the baby, swathed in the bunched-up blanket, as Annie climbed onto the back

seat and settled herself. It wasn't easy maneuvering
in her long dress, hoops and petticoats, especially
after the freedom of the trousers she usually wore.
Annie didn't have much practice in the feminine
arts.

As soon as she stilled on the seat, Josh dumped
the baby in her arms. The back of his hand brushed
her breast. Her eyes came up quickly and met his.
For a second, he didn't move, seemed unable to do
so. Then he turned away and climbed into the seat
ahead of her.

The morning sun was warm, the blue sky cloud-
less and the ride to church silent. For a change, the
three Ingalls children sat quietly, barely moving. After a while, Annie slid her arm around Cassie and
urged her nearer. The child glanced at Ginny in the
seat in front of her, then gave Annie a small smile
and edged closer.

A number of horses, buggies and wagons were
drawn up in the shade of the churchyard. People
milled around, some talking, others already moving
into the church. Reverend Simon, a short, round man
with tufts of white hair ringing his head, stood at
the door, welcoming everyone, shaking hands, nodding politely.

"Wait, children," Annie called as they clambered
out of the surrey.

Holding Hannah on her hip, Annie knelt in front
of the children and appraised them with a critical
eye, smoothing Drew's bangs back off his face and
straightening Cassie's collar.

"Let's all remember to use our Sunday manners today," she told them, then rose and glanced back at Josh. "Be on your best behavior and make your father proud of you."

The children leaned around her, looking at Josh. They seemed less than enthusiastic about Annie's suggestion.

"Let's get inside before services start," Josh said. Apparently he didn't want to walk in late any more than Annie did.

She expected Josh to walk ahead of them, but instead, he hung back and stood next to her.

"Come along, children," Annie said, reaching for Cassie's hand. "We're going to have lots of fun at church today."

But when Annie looked up again, almost everyone in the churchyard had turned to stare, heads bent together. Someone pointed.

Just what she was afraid of.

Annie gulped. Maybe coming to church today had been a mistake, after all.

Chapter Eleven

They could have looked like a normal family, Annie thought, standing at the edge of the churchyard with the baby in her arms, Josh beside her and the three children crowded close.

But Annie was sure none of the people staring at them considered such a thing.

Were they all surprised to see Josh at church, for a change? Were they surprised to see Annie with him? Word might not have spread yet that she was working as his nanny now.

Or were they all thinking of Annie's sister, pregnant and unmarried, and how that reflected on Annie and her family, and now Josh's family, as well?

Josh caught her eye and he, too, seemed uncomfortable with the attention focused on them. Yet perhaps it was something different, Annie thought.

When Josh had last come to church, his wife had been at his side. Lydia Ingalls, the prim and proper lady who wore gowns created by the finest dressmakers on the East Coast and in Europe.

Now, today, he was here with Annie.

She fingered the fabric of her dress. Her blue one. Her favorite. It was nearly as nice as those worn by most of the other settlers, yet far from the fine gowns she imagined Lydia Ingalls had worn. Annie wished she'd taken a little more time in front of the mirror this morning. Wished she felt a little more comfortable in feminine garments.

Someone called to Josh, a man Annie didn't know. He came forward, smiling, offering his hand, and Josh went with him to talk to a group of men standing under one of the trees.

The children spotted friends and hurried away— not asking for permission, of course. Annie couldn't blame them. They probably hadn't seen their friends since school ended in the spring.

Which left Annie standing alone near the Ingalls surrey, holding Hannah, still gathering more attention than she wished for.

Finally, she noticed Camille among the crowd. Relief swamped her as she wound her way toward her sister. Annie was equally pleased, and a little surprised, to see that their mother was there, too.

"Oh, let me have that baby," Sophia crooned, reaching for Hannah with one hand and hugging Annie with the other. "What a beautiful little girl! Tell me all about your new job, Annie. I want to hear everything."

"Oh, Annie, we miss you," Camille declared, wrapping her in a hug. "I can't wait to tell you everything's that happened."

Now Annie wasn't uncomfortable with the stares that still turned their way. All that mattered was that she was with her mother and sister.

"How's Willa?" Annie asked in a low voice. Her sister had come to church only once, when they'd first arrived at the settlement. Since then, with her condition so obvious, she never attended.

"Healthy," Sophia said, rocking Hannah gently in her arms. "But very unhappy. Still crying."

"Any word from Evan Keller or his family?"

"No. Nothing."

The congregation moved toward the church, and Annie and her family fell in with them.

"Mama seems to be feeling better today," Annie whispered as her mother walked in front of them, carrying Hannah and making little cooing noises.

"Since you left to work at the Ingalls farm full-time, she seems to have come around," Camille said. "She's doing much better."

"Thank goodness," Annie said, relieved that not everything had fallen on her younger sister's shoulders since her departure.

"I talked to the schoolmarm about tutoring me, helping me get ready for the Hayden Academy in the fall," Camille said. "Mrs. Hawk is a very nice lady. She offered to help, but she has a new baby now, so she can't spare much time for me."

"What about books? Did she have some that you could study?"

Camille shook her head. "I've worked through all

of the books she has. I don't know what I'm going to do. I haven't much time.''

Annie touched her sister's shoulder. ''You're going to be ready by the time you get to the academy. We'll figure out something.''

Camille smiled, and they walked into church.

As the congregation filled the wooden pews, Annie watched the door for the Ingalls children, fearing she'd end up searching the churchyard for them, demonstrating to the entire settlement just what a poor nanny she was and giving them something else to talk about. But to her relief, all three of them came inside together. Josh was behind them.

''Your family?'' he asked, pulling off his hat, nodding toward her mother and sister already seated on a pew near the back of the church.

''Yes,'' Annie said. ''I'd like to sit with them, if you don't mind.''

''Suits me,'' he said, leaning toward her a little. ''Close to the door.''

The Ingalls family piled into the pew, with Annie seated beside her sister and mother, the children next to her and Josh on the end. Annie made introductions and was a little surprised that Josh spoke so warmly, so politely to her mother and sister. Even the children managed a proper greeting.

As the congregation settled down, Annie craned her neck and located her cousin, Angus Martin, on the other side of the church. A tall, burly man with gray-streaked hair, he'd seated himself about as far away from Annie and her family as he could.

The choir sang the opening hymn, Reverend Simon offered prayer for everyone sick or in need in the settlement, then preached the day's sermon. By the time the offering plate came down the row, the children were starting to squirm and Hannah was getting fussy. At the final prayer, when everyone else had bowed their head, Annie dug into her bag for the baby's bottle and saw that Josh hadn't bowed his head or closed his eyes for the prayer. Instead, he watched a young couple sitting two rows up.

Annie had seem them herself, though she didn't know their names. They'd married only a few weeks ago and, from the looks of things, were still honeymooning.

While everyone else prayed, the two of them snuggled together, gazing into each other's eyes. Sharing a grin, they kissed. What started as a sweet little peck on the lips quickly turned into more. Much more. Mouths grinding together, heavy breathing. Passion.

Yes, definitely passion. It radiated from the young couple. Annie felt it herself, from two rows back. On impulse, she turned to Josh.

He was already looking her way, his cheeks slightly flushed. Their gazes met and held. Josh just looked at her with a slow, steady, unreadable gaze.

Annie stared right back. She couldn't help herself. She felt drawn to Josh, just as the young couple in front of them were drawn to each other.

For a long moment, while Reverend Simon droned on, while somebody coughed and somebody else cleared his throat, she stared at Josh. Finally, Hannah let out a cry that jerked Annie's attention back to her duties.

As she turned to hand the bottle to her mother, she saw that Eleanor Baird—surely the biggest busybody in the settlement—had witnessed their private exchange. Annie cut her gaze away and tended to Hannah, feeling guilty, for some reason.

After church, everyone congregated in the yard again. On some Sundays a social was held after services, but not today. Usually, families invited other families home for supper. Annie and her mother and sister had never been invited home with anyone, and probably never would be.

"Everyone is talking about the big party Mr. Ingalls is having," Sophia said, still holding Hannah, now sleeping in her arms.

Annie had heard other people mention the party this morning, and wasn't sure how the news of the combination harvester's inventor's visit had made the rounds in the settlement already. She guessed that staff at the mercantile had spread the news when Mrs. Flanders had ordered extra supplies for the occasion.

"Everyone is excited," Sophia said. "Seems the parties at Mr. Ingalls's home are something to behold."

"Do you think we could come, too?" Camille asked. "I mean, since you work there now, Annie."

She doubted her position as nanny had done anything to endear her to Mrs. Flanders, much less garner her family a place on the guest list.

"I'll ask," Annie promised.

"Everyone is wondering who will act as Mr. Ingalls's hostess," Sophia said, "now that his wife is gone."

"Hostess?" Annie asked.

"Of course," Sophia said. "Don't tell me you've forgotten such things, Annie. A proper party can't be given without a hostess."

Back in their home in St. Louis, before her father had died, Annie's parents had gone to and given parties of their own. While they were by no means wealthy, Annie's father had been a merchant with a business successful enough to put his family into such circles. Annie, working alongside her mother, had learned the proper way to entertain guests, though she'd never been an enthusiastic student.

Camille glanced around and leaned closer. "I overheard someone say that Eleanor Baird expects Mr. Ingalls will invite her daughter Constance to act as his hostess. See? She's over there now talking to Mr. Ingalls...along with half the settlement."

Annie turned and saw that, indeed, Constance and her mother were among the group of women crowded around Josh, talking, gazing up at him. Josh must have suddenly developed a sense of humor Annie had never witnessed, given all the giggling and eyelash batting that was going on.

And just why that bothered her, Annie didn't know. At once she was hit with the idea of marching

over there, planting herself in the center of the
crowd, at Josh's side. It nearly overcame her.

Yet she couldn't do it. She had no right. Josh
wasn't hers. And, somehow, that made it all the
harder.

Constance was more the type of woman for Josh,
Annie was forced to admit to herself—young, pretty,
wearing a lovely yellow dress that accentuated her
dark eyes and hair. Her family was well off. They
weren't plagued by scandal. Her reputation wasn't
threatened because of it. Constance was just the type
of woman Josh would want.

Without meaning to, Annie found her gaze drifting to Josh. He seemed to sense her, somehow, because he met her eye and shot her a look that cried
out for rescue. Or threatened to throttle her for getting him into this mess. Annie wasn't sure which.
But she had to do something.

"It's getting late. I'd better get the children back
home," Annie said.

"Yes, we should get on our way, too," her
mother said, and gave Hannah a little kiss on the
forehead as she passed her back to Annie.

"Come over this week, when you can," Annie
said to her sister. "We'll have a visit."

"I'd like that," Camille said.

"We'll see," Sophia said, though Annie very
much doubted her mother would ever show up at
the Ingalls house without a formal invitation from
Josh. It wasn't proper, and despite the scandal of her
daughter's pregnancy brewing around her, Sophia

Martin was a proper woman very knowledgeable in the ways of running a home and conducting oneself.

After hugs all around, Annie managed to round up the children, and then approached the circle of women around Josh.

"Excuse me, Mr. Ingalls," she said, refusing to acknowledge any of the cold stares she was getting from the other women. "The children are ready to leave anytime you are."

"Ladies, if you'll excuse me?" Josh said, and shouldered his way out of the gathering.

"But, Mr. Ingalls—"

"Mr. Ingalls—"

Josh shooed the children ahead of them and latched on to Annie's elbow, hurrying across the churchyard toward the surrey.

"Miss Martin," he said, "you're fired."

"Fired? For what?" Annie asked, and would have certainly been alarmed if Josh looked more serious.

"For dragging me here today," he grumbled.

"You're firing me?" Annie tossed her head. "I'd think you'd be *thanking* me."

Josh stopped abruptly and glared down at her. "Thanking you?"

"Yes."

He waved his hand toward the women clustered in the churchyard. "I should thank you? For nearly getting me henpecked to death?"

"For rescuing you. Really, Mr. Ingalls, you should learn to look on the positive side of things more often." Annie dumped Hannah into his arms.

"Here, hold your daughter. And don't wake her up."

She ignored his grumbling as he juggled the baby, turning her attention to the three oldest children, waiting at the surrey. Annie got them loaded, with Cassie on the back seat with her. Josh stood by, awkwardly holding Hannah, huffing impatiently, then thrust her into Annie's arms as soon as she was seated.

Pulling away from the church, Annie couldn't help but notice the gazes following them. Mothers. Young women. Especially Constance Baird.

An odd sense of triumph welled inside Annie. She might not be as pretty as Constance, or dressed as well, or have as much money.

But right now, she was riding away with Josh Ingalls. And Constance was left behind.

The children were a little more talkative on the drive home. Hannah slept the whole way, and Josh said nothing. When they pulled to a stop in front of the house, the children jumped from the surrey. Josh remained behind, helping Annie to the ground.

"I'll get the children settled down for their afternoon nap right away," Annie promised.

Josh's brows pulled together. "Their nap?"

"Yes. Their Sunday afternoon nap. When I was a child we always took a nap on Sunday. I heard several of the men mention it to their wives at church just now."

A grin spread over Josh's face. A big grin that he

fought against, wiggling his mouth and pressing his lips together to contain it.

"What's so funny?" Annie asked. She'd never seen him so amused before.

He cleared his throat, glanced away, then spoke, choosing his words carefully. "A Sunday afternoon nap is more for the benefit of the parents than the children."

"The parents?" she asked, not sure what he meant.

"So they can have some time…together…a-lone…doing husband and wife things."

"Oh." Annie gasped. "Oh!"

Heat roared through her, flaming in her cheeks. She whipped around and ran for the house.

Chapter Twelve

Nighttime at the Ingalls home was lonely. A quiet hung over the house. No servants scurried about doing their chores. No laughter or squeals from the children. Just silence. And loneliness.

At least for Annie.

Alone in her room, she stood at a window looking out at the darkness. She'd thought that going to church this morning would leave her feeling warm and content, after seeing her mother and sister. Instead, it made her miss them more.

True, she'd had a full afternoon taking care of the children. She'd kept busy. Georgia had come and talked to her for a while. Even Mrs. Royce had paused from her cooking to chat for a bit.

But that wasn't enough. They weren't *family*.

Unable to stand the solitude of her room any longer, Annie ventured downstairs. All was quiet, as usual. No one was around, offering any hope for conversation or companionship. No lanterns were lit, except for the faint light beaming from the study.

That was enough.

Annie ventured to the door and looked inside. Josh sat in one of the leather wing chairs that faced the cold hearth, the back of his head visible over the top of the chair.

Annie hesitated at the doorway, not sure if she should disturb him. Unlike her, Josh seemed to enjoy, even treasure solitude.

She debated for a moment, then decided that returning to her empty room, lying in the darkness, staring at nothing, alone with her own thoughts wasn't something she could manage right now. The fact that she'd humiliated herself in front of him when they'd returned from church this morning in that Sunday afternoon nap incident didn't even stop her.

"Mr. Ingalls?" she called.

He scrambled to his feet and turned her way as she walked into the study. He tossed aside the journal he'd been reading. His boots stood beside his chair; a glass of milk sat on the table.

"Is something wrong?" Josh asked. "Are the children all right?"

For a man who seemed to have little interest in his children, Josh's first reaction to seeing her was always that something was wrong with one of them, which Annie found an odd contradiction.

She shook her head. "They're fine. All sleeping soundly."

Despite all the trouble the children caused, they

were good sleepers. At bedtime they stayed in their beds and fell right asleep.

Josh shifted from one foot to the other and glanced down, seemingly embarrassed that she'd caught him in his stocking feet. He'd been less uncomfortable this morning when she'd walked in on him in bed—naked.

Naked.

Annie's mind saw him that way again. Long limbs. Muscles everywhere.

Good gracious, what was wrong with her? She ducked her head, trying desperately to think of something respectable to say.

"I wanted to thank you for taking me to church this morning," she finally said.

Josh nodded. "You're welcome."

Another awkward silence passed.

"I get lonely," Annie said, walking a little farther into the room. "I miss my family. We've always been close, especially since my father died. We've traveled a great deal, lived in quite a few places since we left our home in St. Louis."

"I suppose that's understandable," Josh said.

"Don't you get lonely?"

She expected he'd deny it, or at least tell her it was none of her business, but instead Josh nodded.

"Sometimes," he said.

Lonely for his wife? Annie wondered. She wished she knew, wished desperately he'd give her some sign of his feelings—if any—for his wife.

Instead, he changed the subject. "I didn't mind going to church with you this morning. Not really."

Annie grinned. "So you're not going to fire me?"

"Not today," he answered, then smiled softly.

"Your visit from Mr. Douglas is the talk of the settlement," Annie said. "Seems everyone wants to come to your party."

Josh frowned. "I turned the whole matter over to Mrs. Flanders. She always managed these things, she and...Lydia."

"I'm sure Mrs. Flanders was a tremendous help to your wife."

"Lydia liked things...just so. The house, the meals, the grounds, the children," Josh said. "Everything."

He seemed to get lost in his thoughts, his memories. Annie couldn't help but wonder what else "everything" entailed.

For a moment, she considered slipping away, leaving him alone with whatever had claimed his attention. But something inside her wouldn't let her leave. Something told her he needed a distraction.

Annie gestured to the bookshelves. "Would you mind loaning a few of your books to my sister? She's very studious. She'll take good care of them, I promise you that."

"Your sister Camille?"

Annie nodded, a little surprised that he remembered her sister's name after their brief meeting in church this morning.

"There's only the two of you?" Josh asked. "You and Camille?"

A little knot tightened Annie's throat. Great. Just what she needed, a discussion of her family.

"As I said, we're a small family," Annie told him, skirting the issue. "So, do you mind if she comes over and borrows some of your books?"

"No, I don't mind. Someone should get use out of these things. I certainly don't have time to read them. I'll help you pick out something," Josh offered.

Annie walked to the wall of books with Josh behind her. In the faint lantern light, the titles were difficult to read. She moved closer. So did he.

Heat from his body wafted over her, seeped into her. The scent of him came with it, bringing all her own senses to life.

"Let's see," Josh mused. "What would be appropriate for your sister?"

His voice was at her ear, mellow and rich. His breath puffed warmly against her. Annie trembled.

Josh couldn't remember when this wall of books had seemed so enticing. When the room had smelled so good. When he'd felt this overwhelming urge to—

To what?

Standing behind Annie and slightly to the side, he glanced down at her. Lantern light made her skin seem to glow as she gazed intently at the books, her face upturned, her eyes wide, her lips slightly parted. She still had on the dress she'd worn to church this morning, and her hair was twisted atop her head. A few tendrils had come loose, curling against her neck.

Her neck. Her soft neck. And her shoulder. All right there. Inches away. Begging for him to—

To what?

Josh cleared his throat and focused his attention on the books again. "Do you think she'd like something by James Fenimore Cooper?"

"Well…"

"Charles Dickens?"

"I think something instructional would be more appropriate."

"I have all four volumes of Audubon's *The Birds of America*."

"Yes, she should definitely read those." Annie tilted her head, looking for the books on the shelves.

"Right there," Josh said, reaching around her to point out the volumes on a higher shelf.

"Perfect," she said. "I'll just—"

He kissed her on the neck. She rose on her toes to fetch the books and Josh leaned down and placed his lips against the flesh of her neck. He hadn't meant to, certainly hadn't intended to, but now couldn't stop himself.

Josh moved his lips against her, tasting her, breathing in her scent. Then, to his amazement, Annie moved her head to the side, ever so slightly. An invitation? Josh's blood pumped hotter and faster.

He eased his hands to her waist, drawing her closer, and moved his mouth down her neck to the top of her shoulder, exposed by her dress. Sweet. She tasted sweet and warm and alive.

Annie turned to face him, her legs barely able to hold her upright, and caught his arms to steady herself. His lips had touched only a small part of her, yet she tingled everywhere.

Then he kissed her on the mouth. Their lips met and blended together, making Annie's head spin. Josh pushed deeper and she let him. He slipped his tongue inside her, filling her with warmth and a hunger she'd never imagined.

He eased her back against the bookcase and pressed his body closer, barely brushing hers. Heat rose between them. She curled her fingers into the fabric of his shirt.

Finally, he groaned softly and lifted his head. Annie held tight, fearing she'd fall. For a long moment they simply gazed at each other in the lamplight. Her heart pounded in her chest. His breathing was quick and hot.

"Are you going to apologize for this tomorrow?" Annie asked him.

"Only if you feel I should…if you feel that it lacks passion, again."

"Well, we'll have to see," Annie whispered. "I'll think it over and let you know."

"Is that so?" he asked, grinning.

"That's so," she told him.

Josh stepped back, allowing cooling air to swirl between them, yet looking as if he wanted to move closer instead, perhaps kiss her again. In that instant,

Annie knew that if he wanted to kiss her again, she'd let him. Because she wanted it, too.

Instead, she skirted around him and hurried out of the study.

Upstairs in her room, Annie flung open the window and undressed quickly, tossing aside petticoats, corset, hoops, until she stood in only her pantalets and chemise in the cooling night air.

What was she thinking? She shouldn't have kissed Josh. She was his children's nanny. And she certainly shouldn't have kissed him in the study. Her family was already awash with scandal. What if one of the servants had walked in on them?

Still, she trembled with the memory of his embrace, his mouth. She still tasted his lips on hers. Felt the heat of his kiss against her neck.

She'd never been kissed like that before. Even when he'd kissed her in the field, she hadn't experienced the physical energy Josh had given off as she had in his study just now.

Was that what she was feeling? The satisfaction of her own curiosity about such things?

Or was it more?

"Mind your own business," Annie muttered, and pulled her night rail from the drawer.

If she wanted to keep her job, she'd best mind her own business. And her own business definitely did not include kissing her employer.

No matter how good it felt.

Chapter Thirteen

What was wrong with him? What the hell was wrong with him?

Josh banged out the back door, grumbling under his breath, striding across the yard.

He'd overslept, and he never overslept. He'd tossed and turned all night, when he usually slept like a log. He'd flopped around on the bed, tangled the covers, gotten up to straighten them, paced the floor, opened and closed the window a half-dozen times.

Then when he'd finally—finally—fallen asleep just before dawn, he'd had most vivid, the most lurid dreams since—

Josh pulled at the tight muscles of his neck. Hell, he couldn't remember ever having such dreams.

Just days ago he'd been troubled over the recurring dream about Night Hawk and an eagle. But last night had nothing to do with either of them, and everything to do with—

He stopped abruptly. No. It had nothing to do with *her*. Even if she was in the dream. Even if—

What the hell was wrong with him?

Josh stalked toward the corral, tired from not getting enough sleep and filled with pent-up energy that had to be spent. Somehow. On something. On someone.

"Damn..."

Annie popped into his mind again, just as she'd floated through his dreams last night. His footsteps slowed as he recalled the image of her his mind had conjured up while he slept. Annie with her—

"Damn!"

Josh picked up his pace again, anxious to begin the day's work that lay ahead. Anxious for the distraction from his own thoughts. He hadn't bothered with breakfast, just wolfed down a biscuit on his way through the cookhouse, feeling the stares from Mrs. Royce as he went out the door.

He didn't want to talk to anyone, didn't want to see anyone this morning. Not friends, servants, children or Annie.

Especially not Annie.

The last thing he needed right now was to lay eyes on her and be reminded again of how he'd kissed her in his study last night. How he'd dreamed about her. How merely the thought of her made him want to—

A rooster tail of dust drew Josh's attention to the winding road that led to his farm. He squinted at the approaching buggy.

He couldn't quite make out the faces of the visitors intending to pay a call on him, but he recognized the buggy easily. The Bairds. And the two women seated behind the driver had to be Eleanor and her daughter Constance.

"Damn…"

Josh was not going to suffer through a visit from those two women. No way in hell. Not today. Not in the mood he was in.

The children were gone—again. Thanks to Mrs. Flanders—again.

Annoyed, Annie climbed down the rickety ladder from the barn's loft, where she'd spent the last few minutes looking for them. No sign of the children up there. No sign of them anywhere.

When she reached the dirt floor, Annie brushed off her hands and swiped straw from her shirt; she'd given up trying to wear a dress during the day.

First thing this morning, Mrs. Flanders had made a point of stopping Annie in the hallway and telling her that she had, yet again, given the children permission to leave the house. Annie had been so angry she'd barely contained her temper. But she'd managed to, fearing that was exactly what Mrs. Flanders wanted.

She didn't know why, but it appeared as if the housekeeper didn't like her, didn't want her to succeed at her job. Annie didn't know the reason, and at the moment, didn't care to know it. All she cared about was finding the children. She'd been content to let them have their way while she got to know Hannah better and acclimated herself to the house and grounds.

But enough was enough. If she had any hope of keeping her job, Annie had to have some sort of control over the children.

Georgia had been kind enough to keep an ear out for Hannah after Annie put her down for her morning nap, and she'd come outside to search. So far, she'd looked in most of the outbuildings and the gardens, tromped through the meadow and had even gone down to the stream, but hadn't found them. She'd just checked the barn again, thinking they might have doubled back.

But, to her dismay, no one was in the barn. Not even any livestock. The horses were in the adjoining corral. Still, the place smelled of the animals, and of leather, dirt, straw and grain. Not altogether unpleasant scents.

Annie blew out a breath, ready to give up her search and admit defeat, when the barn's side door jerked open and Josh jumped inside. He spun, slammed the door and fell against it.

A few seconds passed while he just stood there, still and silent. Then he turned slowly, opened the door a crack and peeked out.

"What are you doing?"

He slammed the door again, then searched the barn's dim interior until he spotted her.

"Nothing," he said.

Annie almost laughed in his face, he looked so

guilty, his claim of innocence such a blatant lie. And she knew it was a lie because she'd seen that same look on the faces of his three oldest children.

"You're hiding from someone," she realized, seeing his palm still pressed against the coarse wood of the door.

"No, I'm not," Josh told her. He sounded guiltier every time he spoke.

She walked over. "Then you won't mind if I go outside and—"

Josh reached over her head and held the door closed. He glared down at her. Annie folded her arms and drummed her fingers against her elbow, raising her brows at him.

"Okay, you're right," he admitted. "There's someone outside I don't want to talk to."

"Who?" Annie tugged on the door handle, suddenly intrigued and dying to know who it was that sent Josh Ingalls—the wealthiest, most powerful man in the settlement —running for cover.

"Never mind who," he told her, still holding the door closed.

"I want to know," she insisted.

"Shh! Keep quiet."

Annie straightened her shoulders. "Not until you tell me who it is."

Josh grumbled a curse, then huffed. "All right. It's those Baird women."

Annie gasped. This wasn't funny anymore.

He opened the door a crack and tilted his head,

trying to see through it. "I saw their buggy just now coming up drive."

"Eleanor Baird?"

"Yes." He pressed his face against the wood, peering out.

"Eleanor Baird? The biggest gossip in the settlement?"

"Yes."

"Quite possibly the biggest gossip in the whole state of Wisconsin?"

"Yes," he insisted, still looking out.

"*And* her daughter?"

"Yes! Now keep your voice down before they—"

"Out of my way!"

Annie pushed him, and because she'd caught him off guard, shoved him back a step. She grabbed the door handle and yanked. He slammed it shut again.

"You can't go out there," he told her. "They'll see you and—"

"I am not about to be found closeted away in the barn with you," she told him, "not with those two women out there to witness the whole thing."

"We won't be found if you'll just keep quiet," he barked, and planted himself between her and the door.

"Move!" She shoved him again, but this time got nowhere. Still, she wasn't about to give up.

Annie tried a different tact. "Look, just let me leave. You can hide in here all day, for all I care."

"No," Josh insisted, peeking out the door again. "You'll draw attention."

"That's your problem," she told him. "Now, if you don't get out of my way—"

"Damn!" Josh pushed the door closed and looked back at her. "Here comes one of the servants. That old battle-ax Mrs. Baird probably sent her looking for me."

"Who is it?"

Annie squirmed in front of him. She looked out as he opened the door a crack, and saw Georgia walking toward the barn.

"I'll talk to her," Annie said. "I'll tell her you've ridden out to the field already."

"Forget it."

"But—"

Josh's arm closed around her waist, lifted off her feet and deposited her behind him. "You're not telling her anything. She won't believe you."

Annie straightened. "Of course she will."

"She won't." Josh looked back at her. "You're the worst liar I've seen in my entire life."

Annie flung out her arms. "Oh, well, excuse me if my lying skills aren't up to your high standards!"

"Shh!" Josh peered out again. "Damn, she's coming this way. Come on!"

Annie stood her ground. "I am not going anywhere!"

"And I am not going to spend my entire afternoon cooped up in the parlor, listening to that woman rattle on and on for hours about nothing, while that daughter of hers giggles and bats her eye-lashes at me!'' Josh grabbed her arm. ''Come on!''

Annie pulled against him and dug in her heels. She was not—absolutely not—going to take the chance of being discovered hiding in the barn with Josh. Not by Eleanor Baird.

Soft singing drifted through the barn door. Georgia. Josh looked at Annie, and they both turned toward the sound. She was getting closer.

Annie opened her mouth to protest again, but Josh scooped her up and hurried to the stall at the farthest end of the barn. When Josh set her down, Annie made a break for it. Their feet tangled. Down they went into the hay.

''Mr. Ingalls?''

Josh threw one leg over Annie's to still her thrashing, caught both of her hands in one of his and covered her mouth with his other palm.

''Mr. Ingalls, you in here?'' Georgia called.

Annie quieted, quelling the urge to bite his hand. Now she didn't dare be discovered. Good gracious, how would this look? It was bad enough that she could have been found alone in the barn with Josh; now she'd be caught rolling around in the hay with him.

''Yoo-hoo! Mr. Ingalls?'' Georgia yelled. ''You got company up at the house! You in here?''

Footsteps scuffling through the dirt came their way. Annie held her breath. Josh leaned down, flattening himself against her.

He pulled his hand from her mouth. They both

lay perfectly still, ears straining. Annie didn't know about Josh, but she said a prayer.

Moments dragged by, enough that she became fully aware of Josh's weight on her. His thigh over her legs. His fingers gripping her hands. His tempered strength, his power, as he exuded just enough control to keep her still but not hurt her.

Annie turned her head toward him. He looked down at her. His mouth hovered inches from hers. He drew nearer, nearer—

"Well, tarnation." Georgia's voice drifted over them, coming from farther away, and she muttered to herself as her footsteps faded. Finally, the barn door closed.

But Josh didn't move. He didn't get up. Didn't let Annie get up, either. He held her beneath him and lowered his mouth to hers until—

"Get off of me!" Annie swatted at him, kicked and squirmed until he rolled away. She sat up, catching her breath, gathering her composure.

Annie looked back at Josh. He watched her, braced on one arm, one knee drawn up, the other leg outstretched. She turned away again.

"I'm leaving," she told him, "and I want you to stay in this barn for at least fifteen minutes so no one knows, or even suspects, that we were in here together."

She almost wished he'd protest, because she was in a mood and it suited her just fine to take it out on him. But Josh said nothing, so Annie shoved herself to her feet.

"Wait." Josh got up and came after her.

She whirled. "I'm leaving this minute and there's nothing you can do to stop me."

"You have straw on your..." Josh waved his hands toward her bottom.

Annie looked down at herself, then at him and gasped. They were both covered with straw.

"Good gracious," she said, swatting at the straw, "we may as well take off our trousers and wave them from the loft window!"

"Here, let me—" Josh offered, reaching for her.

"Don't touch me!" she told him.

"I was only trying to help."

"Don't help me, either."

Josh cursed softly and flapped his hands uselessly at his sides.

"It's not like we actually *did* anything," he said, and sounded slightly offended. "You're carrying on as if we'd shared some grand, passionate moment."

"You just keep to yourself from now on. And if you're able to work up any of this grand passion you're claiming to possess, I'll thank you to direct it to your children! Or your own life! Or something other than me!"

Annie stormed out of the barn.

Chapter Fourteen

Had she accused him of having no passion?

Josh had mulled that question over in his mind for most of the day while he'd ridden restlessly over his farm, and even after he'd joined his field workers in their backbreaking labor, which had lasted until after sundown. Then he'd spent an undue amount of time tending to his horse, finding busywork, wandering around, thinking.

Of course he had passion, Josh told himself, as he left the barn and headed toward the house. He was passionate about a lot of things—his farm, his crops, his…farm. His crops…

"Hell…"

Josh stepped into the cookhouse through the outside door and headed to the little room built on the end, where the family bathed. It held a tub, a pump, a stove for winter, and cupboards. The room had been Lydia's idea, intended primarily as a place where Josh was to bathe and change his clothes after

working all day, before he entered the main house.
She saw to it that he always had clean clothing waiting, whatever she wanted him to wear for the evening.

In the months since her death, he'd gotten out of
the habit. Now he just washed up. He seldom took
the time to bathe and change, unless he really
needed to.

And this evening, he really needed to.

Even working in the fields all day hadn't worn
down the tension simmering inside him. Josh
pumped the tub full of cold water, not bothering to
heat it on the stove, then stripped off his clothes and
sank into it, thinking it might help.

It didn't.

Nothing helped. He couldn't get his mind off Annie. And his body's reaction to those thoughts
wasn't helping matters.

Clean, dry and dressed in fresh clothes, Josh left
the bathing room. Delicious smells filled the cookhouse as Mrs. Royce and her helpers busied themselves at the stove and worktables. The women were
always busy. He didn't know what they did, or why,
or how his family possibly consumed the massive
quantities of food they cooked; Lydia had always
handled the cooks.

"Evening, Mr. Ingalls," Mrs. Royce said. "I've
kept your supper warm for you. Are you ready to
eat, sir?"

"Later," he said, and kept walking.

"Yes, sir, I understand," she said, though the

look on her face indicated just the opposite. Meals in the Ingalls household had always been served on a schedule; the cook didn't seem to know what to make of this unexpected departure.

Really, Josh didn't know, either.

"Where's Annie?" he asked.

"Upstairs, I think, sir," Mrs. Royce replied.

He bounded up the back staircase to the second floor. The only lamplight spilling into the hallway was from the children's room. Standing in the shadow, he saw Annie with Hannah on her hip, moving about the room, getting the other children settled into bed.

She moved with an easy grace, even carrying the baby. In fact, little Hannah in her arms only added to her artful movements.

With one hand Annie pulled back the covers, waited patiently until each child climbed under, then spread the coverlets up. She offered to read a story, but Ginny told her no. Annie touched Cassie's cheek, then turned down the wall lantern and disappeared through the door to the adjoining nursery.

Josh stood in the dim light looking at his children, tiny bulges under their covers. They spoke softly. Such sweet voices. He couldn't make out the words.

Before, Lydia had had the nanny bring them downstairs to him at bedtime. Each child had given him a kiss on the cheek and said good-night before being whisked upstairs again.

He'd stopped doing that, too, after Lydia's death.

It reminded him too much of her, and made him think of…well, made him think of too many things.

Josh listened at the doorway for a while longer until the children quieted, then walked to the balcony at the back of the house. He stood at the railing and looked out over his farm.

The air was cool and smelled rich and sweet. Darkness spread across the land and blended into the sky, speckled with stars. Birds sang their night songs.

Occasionally, he glanced over his shoulder, watching for Annie. He wasn't sure how long it took to get the baby settled and asleep in her crib.

It was doubtful that Annie would go down to his study tonight, as she had before. After this morning in the barn, he figured he was the last person she'd come looking for this evening—or perhaps ever again. He kept an eye on her closed bedroom door.

After a while, the door opened and Annie walked out. She didn't even pause at the top of the staircase. As he'd suspected, she had no intention of venturing downstairs. Instead she walked toward the balcony—and him.

Josh stepped deeper into the shadows as she approached. She drew in a big breath and let it out slowly. Annie smoothed her hair back, then planted her hands on the railing and looked out.

Lord, she was pretty. Josh knew he should call her name and make his presence known immediately, but he indulged himself for a moment and kept looking at her.

Pretty. Natural. Simple. That was Annie. Not made up, trussed up, dressed up like so many other women. And the best part of it was that she looked so comfortable as she was.

Those trousers. Josh's blood began to pump a little faster. Lord, could Annie wear a pair of trousers. There was nothing mannish about Annie in trousers. Not with those long, long legs. That trim waist. Those curves and swells and—

"Mr. Ingalls? Is that you?"

Annie was facing him now, tilting her head for a better look.

Josh cleared his throat and stepped into the faint light that spilled from the wall lanterns in the hallway. "Yes, it's me."

"Are you all right? I heard you moan."

"I didn't—well, I might have—" Josh cleared his throat again and pulled on the back of his neck. "Anyway, I came to talk to you, to ask you a question."

She frowned suspiciously and stood a little straighter, as if bracing herself. "What sort of question?"

Josh walked closer and stood at the railing next to her. "This morning in the barn, did you mean it when you said you thought I had no passion?"

Annie's expression soured and she turned away sharply, gazing across the farm. "I have no recollection of any such conversation."

"No?" He leaned to the left, catching her eye. "No."

"Surely you remember being in the barn? You and me in the farthest stall, my leg thrown over you, you lying with your—"

"Shh!" Annie glanced back toward the house, then waved her hands at him. "Keep you voice down, for heaven's sake. Yes, all right, I remember. Of course I remember."

"Well? Did you mean it? Do you think I have no passion?"

"I'm not going to answer that question."

"Why not?"

"Because I want to keep my job," she told him.

Josh frowned. "I wouldn't fire you for expressing your opinion."

"You haven't heard my opinion yet."

Josh shifted his shoulders and rolled his neck, loosening his tight muscles. "I guess I have my answer."

He leaned his elbow on the railing, easing closer to her. "Do you think I lack passion because I didn't kiss you this morning in the barn?"

She looked up sharply. "No."

"Are you disappointed that I didn't kiss you?"

Her mouth gaped open, then snapped shut. Regally, she turned her head away. "Of course not."

"Then what makes you think I lack passion?"

Annie sighed heavily. "Look, Mr. Ingalls, I—"

"Josh," he told her. "If two people are discussing passion, they ought to be on a first-name basis, don't you think? Annie?"

She seemed to melt, just a little. The icy mantle

she'd wrapped herself in dissolved for a fraction of a second. Annie gazed up at him, her eyes sparkling like the stars above. Then, as quickly, they clouded over and she turned away.

"No, I don't think we should be on a first-name basis," she told him, "and I don't think we should be discussing passion. Certainly not yours. Unless it's for your children, which I'd like to see you actually work up."

Josh straightened, unprepared and a little surprised by the anger in her voice.

"What have the children got to do with anything?" he asked.

"That's exactly my point," Annie told him. "You don't talk to them, you don't eat with them, you don't tuck them in at night, you don't have anything to do with them. Why?"

"Because *you're* here. That's what *you're* supposed to do."

"I'm just their nanny."

"And I'm just their father." Anger welled inside Josh, more welcome than the other emotions he'd wrestled with lately. "You're supposed to do all those things. That's why I hired you. That's what nannies do."

"Says who?"

Josh flung out his arms. What the hell was she talking about? "That's the way it's done. That's the way it's always been done."

Annie pressed her lips together. "And that's all right with you?"

He pushed his fingers through his hair. "Why wouldn't it be?"

"Fine." Annie spat the word at him, spun around and marched across the balcony. She stopped at the door. "I just hope your decision will keep you company in your old age and keep you warm at night."

She stomped inside.

Josh let loose a mouthful of curses and bounced his fist off the balcony railing. What the hell had just happened? What the hell was she talking about?

And why did he want to kiss her again?

"You should have minded your own business," Annie mumbled to herself as she climbed the stairs.

What had she been thinking, butting into Josh's business? Speaking her mind. Shouting at him. Criticizing how he wanted his children raised. And telling him, of all things, that he had no passion in his life. How could she have said those things?

Even if they were all true.

Since their confrontation on the balcony several days ago, Annie hadn't spoken to Josh. Or rather, he hadn't spoken to her.

She'd seen him a few times in the house, or riding out to the fields. She was certain he'd seen her, too. But not once had he tried to talk to her. He'd not even nodded his head or lifted his lips in a smile. Nothing. He ignored her.

Probably afraid that if he acknowledged her presence, she'd let loose with another round of "good advice."

Annie paused in the upstairs hallway and considered whether or not she should go down and apologize to Josh. He was in his study, as he usually was this time of night. She'd seen the lantern light glowing from the room before she'd come up to retire for the evening.

Maybe she should do just that. Go to Josh and apologize. Tell him she was sorry. Promise to mind her own business from now on.

The only problem with that idea was that she wasn't sorry for what she'd said. Not at all. Not a word of it.

And, surely, Josh would realize she wasn't being truthful. He'd said she was the worst liar he'd seen in his entire life. He'd told her to her face that morning in the barn.

Annie's heart beat a little faster at the recollection. How empty the barn had been until he'd burst through the door. How his presence seemed to fill it to the rafters. Then he'd swept her into his arms and carried her into the stall. His leg across hers. His hands gripping hers. The smell of him, the strength, the power. She'd thought he'd kiss her, lying together in the hay. For a moment, she'd wanted him to, hadn't cared that they might be caught, had given no thought to the scandal that would follow, if that happened.

Then she'd come to her senses. What little was left of them.

Annie blew out a heavy breath. Certainly, no one could accuse *her* of having no passion.

And all of hers had been directed at the children, these past few days, anyway.

She tiptoed to their doorway and listened to the sounds of their slumbers. Thank goodness they were sleeping.

Though she hadn't thought it possible, their behavior had worsened. They'd gone from running off during the day to creating all sorts of mischief. They'd overturned the feed barrels, raided the henhouse and had an egg fight, dumped a bucket of mud on the cookhouse worktable to make mud pies, damaged some of the farm equipment and broken a figurine on a downstairs table running through the house this afternoon.

Annie shuddered to think what they might get into next, what—or who—might be their next target.

She went into her own room, lit the lantern and closed the door. She was tired. Hannah had taken to waking during the night, so Annie had slept little lately. She was anxious to fall into bed and, hopefully, stay there until morning. If little Hannah would cooperate.

She'd started to undress when a knock sounded on her door. She opened it and found Georgia standing in the hallway looking worried.

"What'd you do?" Georgia asked in a low voice.

Alarm spread through Annie. Georgia, who took the ups and downs of life in the Ingalls house in stride, looked grim.

"I didn't do anything."

"You musta' went and did something," Georgia said, shaking her head sorrowfully. "Because Mr. Ingalls wants to see you. Right now. And let me tell you, Annie, he don't look happy."

Chapter Fifteen

"What did he say?" Annie asked, more annoyed than worried that she'd been called downstairs.

"He just said for me to come and get you. He didn't tell me nothing 'bout nothing." Georgia looked up and down the hall, then lowered her voice. "All I can tell you is that I saw ol' Mrs. Flanders in his study with him, and they'd been talking for a while."

"Great…"

"You sure you didn't do something?" Georgia asked, leaning closer.

Annie shook her head. "I'm positive."

"What about the kids?"

Annie frowned. "What *haven't* they done?"

Georgia pressed her lips together. "You reckon he's a-gonna fire you?"

"I guess I'll find out." Annie summoned what strength she could and headed down the stairs.

She expected to find Mrs. Flanders in the study

alongside Josh, but he was alone, seated at his desk, looking over a ledger.

How handsome he looked, Annie thought, stepping into the room. Elbow on the desk, cheek propped on his palm, staring thoughtfully at the page in front of him. How handsome he looked—getting ready to fire her?

"Mr. Ingalls?" she called.

His head jerked up and he came to his feet, standing straight. "Come in." He sounded formal and reserved. Very businesslike.

Annie's stomach knotted in dread. He was going to fire her.

"I need to speak to you," Josh told her.

Beg.

Weary as she was, the idea flashed in Annie's mind as she approached his desk with him standing formidably behind it. Beg. Beg for her job. She needed the money to send Camille away to school, to help with her mother's living expenses, buy things Willa would need for the new baby. She needed this job.

Yet something inside Annie wouldn't let her do it. She wouldn't beg. Not from Josh.

Annie steeled herself and stopped in front of his desk.

"It's come to my attention that the children caused some mischief today," Josh said. "I want to know what happened."

Gracious, where to start? The mud pies, the damaged farm equipment, the egg fight?

When she didn't answer immediately, Josh frowned. "Mrs. Flanders told me what happened this afternoon. I want your side of it."

"My side?"

"Yes. I want to hear your account of the incident. I want to be fair."

How strange it felt standing across the desk from him, staring into his stern face, feeling slightly intimidated, when only days ago he'd kissed her in this very room. He'd have kissed her again in the barn, if she'd let him.

Josh certainly didn't want to kiss her now.

Still, he'd managed to raise a whole series of emotions in her at the moment. She wanted to melt into his arms, lay her head on that broad chest of his and rest. Yet another side of her grew angry at the distance he seemed to be putting between the two of them at the moment.

He hadn't spoken to her in days. He'd kissed her twice, risked ruining her reputation in the barn, wanted to discuss his passion—of all things—with her, then ignored and avoided her for days. And now—now—all he wanted to talk about was the children's behavior?

"I suppose that if it was Mrs. Flanders who spoke with you it must have been about the figurine that was broken," Annie said, and heard the tinge of anger in her voice.

He frowned. "Was there something else?"

Did he really not know what other problems his children had caused today? Or all the other days before that? Had his foreman and workers kept the children's pranks to themselves, and only Mrs. Flanders told on them?

Apparently so. Another tremor of anger rose in Annie. How like Mrs. Flanders to make an issue of it.

"No," Annie told him. "There was nothing else."

Josh looked irritated. She'd forgotten for a moment that he claimed he could tell when she was lying.

"Nothing you need to concern yourself with," Annie amended.

"If the children are too much for you—"

"They're not."

"If they're misbehaving, I'll punish them."

"Punish them?" Annie's anger grew tenfold. "You'll punish them? You won't talk with them, eat with them, play with them, but you'll take the time to punish them?"

Josh just stared at her, as if he didn't understand what she was saying, what she meant. Or why she was angry.

Gracious, she'd done it again. Overstepped her bounds. Butted in. Annie rushed ahead.

"Hannah is teething. She requires more of my attention. I wasn't supervising the children as closely as I should have and they ran through the house, bumped the table and broke the figurine. It was my fault for not watching them more closely. I'll do better in the future."

Annie lowered her gaze, trying to look and sound contrite, and pressed her lips together in an attempt to keep the rest of her comments to herself and control her seething anger.

"Hannah is getting a tooth?"

She raised her eyes quickly, stunned by his comment. "Yes, her first."

Josh looked mildly pleased. "Which one?"

"Bottom front."

"I suppose that's why I've heard her crying so often during the night."

Annie resisted the urge to tell him that it would have been nice if he'd gotten up to tend to his own daughter one of those times so she could have gotten a little sleep.

"You can take the cost of the figurine out of my pay," Annie told him, anxious to end this conversation before she blurted out something that got her fired.

He shook his head. "No, I won't do that."

"It's only fair. It was my fault, my responsibility," Annie said, feeling more irritable.

"No."

"I insist."

"No."

"But—"

"I'd have to give you a raise before you could afford to replace it."

Annie jerked back, feeling as if she'd been slapped. Another reminder that she was an employee here, a servant from a simple family, lucky to have this job. Heat flashed through her, warming her cheeks, but taking away none of her anger.

Josh shifted uncomfortably and glanced away. He softened his voice. "From now on, if there's a problem with the children, I'd prefer to hear about it from you, rather than Mrs. Flanders."

"I'm not going to do that." Annie hit him with the words like a shotgun blast.

His expression hardened. "Why not?"

Because she wanted to handle the children herself. She wanted their respect and their obedience because she'd earned it. Because it was her job. Not because Josh would punish them.

"I'm not going to run to you with every little thing that comes along," Annie told him. "You have enough to do without spending your evenings hearing how poorly your children behave. They are my responsibility and I will handle them."

"But I want you to tell me."

"I won't!"

Josh pulled in a breath, holding down his temper. "I know that those children—"

"*Your* children?"

"Yes, *my* children can be a handful. Have you read the book I gave you? The one on child rearing?"

Annie's eyes widened. "That's your solution? That I should read a book?"

"It's a highly respected book. Are you using it?"

"Yes! It makes a terrific doorstop! Now I can

hear Hannah cry quite clearly during the night, thank you very much!''

''Those are my children, and I insist that I—''

''Oh, really? *Now* they're *your* children?'' Annie waved her hands. ''For your information, Mr. Ingalls, you can't pick and choose when it suits you to be involved in their upbringing! It doesn't work that way!''

''I will have a say—''

''No! I've got more than enough interference in my duties as it is,'' Annie told him. ''If you really want to have some involvement, then tell the rest of the staff to leave the children to me! *That* is what you can do for your children!''

Annie whipped around and left the room.

Josh stared after her, his jaw going slack. What the hell had just happened? He felt as if he'd been caught flat-footed in a twister.

And who the hell did she think she was? No one—not even Lydia had ever shouted at him.

Josh dropped into his chair. Lydia. Certainly, never Lydia...

For a moment he considered that he'd been better off with the string of nannies who'd been after him for his money. Annie taxed him in so many other ways.

And just why she had been angry with him he wasn't sure. He'd called her down to his study to hear her side of what had happened with the children today, hadn't simply believed the things Mrs. Flanders had told him. He'd offered to punish the children. What was so wrong with that? That's what he was supposed to do. That's what he had always done in the past.

Drumming his fingers on his desk, Josh felt his anger drain away. Annie looked a little tired. If she'd been up at night with Hannah, it was no wonder she was grumpy and on edge.

When he'd heard the baby crying these past few nights, he'd simply put another pillow over his head and gone back to sleep. Annie hadn't had that luxury. She'd had to get up with her. Stayed up God knows how long.

Still, that was no excuse for shouting at him. After all, he was in charge of the house. It was his home, his farm, his children, and Annie was his employee.

Josh pushed himself to his feet. He needed to set things straight. He wouldn't tolerate such insubordination. He'd go up to her room right now and—

"Oh, God..." He sank into his chair again.

Visions floated through his head. Annie upstairs. In her night rail. In her trousers. In the barn...with him. Him lying beside her in the hay. Him wanting to—

Josh lurched out of his chair. He'd never get a wink of sleep tonight entertaining thoughts like this, and he had too much to do tomorrow to toss and turn for hours not getting the rest he needed.

Banishing thoughts of Annie, Annie's trousers, Annie's night rail, the barn and his own wants from his mind, Josh blew out the lantern and headed upstairs.

* * *

Annie pushed herself out of bed, one eye barely opened, and lurched across the room toward the sound of Hannah's cries.

She didn't know what time it was, only that it was the middle of the night. No moonbeams streamed in through the windows. Only the thin lamplight from the nursery guided her toward the door.

Annie pushed her hair back over her shoulder as she felt her way along the wall, past the desk to the doorway, so tired and sleepy that she still couldn't open her other eye. She groped her way into the nursery toward the crib.

Her hand landed on flesh. Hard, hot flesh. A mountain of it.

Both of Annie's eyes sprang open and she saw Josh standing at the baby's crib, and her hand splayed across his back.

He'd pulled on trousers, but that was all. His chest was bare, the crinkly hair glinting in the lantern light as he held Hannah against him, tangled in her blanket.

"Sorry," he said in a low voice, just loud enough to be heard over Hannah's fussing. "I didn't mean to frighten you."

"No, it's—it's all right," Annie stammered, pulling her hand away, feeling her fingers tingle, trying to get her groggy brain to work. "It's just that I...what are you doing in here?"

"I heard her crying," Josh said, juggling Hannah awkwardly.

"Oh. Sorry she disturbed you."

"It's all right. I wasn't sleeping, anyway," Josh said, and he glanced at Annie, giving her a quick sweep that took her in from her bare toes to the top of her toussled head. "You'd said you hadn't gotten much sleep lately, so when I heard Hannah crying I thought I'd take care of her."

Her brows crept upward. "Really?"

"Only, now that I'm here," Josh said, looking pained, "I don't know what the hell I'm supposed to do with her."

"The same as you did for the three older children," Annie said.

Josh looked totally lost now.

"Don't you remember the others teething?" Annie asked.

"No," he admitted. "The nanny took care of things like that...I guess."

Annie smiled. "What a treat you've missed."

"Well, what am I supposed to do?"

Where a woman holding a crying baby would naturally sway from side to side, Josh stood rigid and still.

"Rock her," Annie said. "And hold her close to you. Put your arms around her. She'll feel secure."

"Uh, well, all right." He moved the baby against his shoulder and wrapped both arms around her, watching Annie as she opened a drawer in the bureau. "I don't think this is working."

"Give it a few minutes," Annie said, taking out a small jar. "And this will help."

"What is it?"

"Something to make her gums stop hurting. Mrs. Royce made it up for me. Honey, herbs, a little whiskey."

Annie rubbed some on Hannah's gums while Josh held her and watched. "She'll settle down in a few minutes," Annie said, wiping off her hand. "Hold her against you."

Josh pulled the baby onto his shoulder again.

"Rock her."

He swayed back and forth, a little faster than was necessary. "I don't seem to have any natural instincts for this sort of thing."

Annie smiled. "You're doing fine."

Gradually, Hannah stopped fussing, but showed no signs of falling back to sleep.

"Do you ever put her in bed with you?" Josh asked.

"It's not a good idea."

Josh raised his brows. "You're particular about who gets into bed with you?"

She blushed at the highly personal question, but couldn't let it go. "Actually, I am."

He grinned. "Actually, I'm rather glad to hear it."

Annie cheeks colored deeper and she changed the subject. "In this case, chances are that if Hannah sleeps with me one night, she'll want to sleep there every night."

"I can understand that," Josh said, stifling a smile, trying to look serious.

"Put her back in her crib," Annie said. "Usually, she'll go back to sleep on her own."

After more awkward shifting and juggling, Josh got the baby settled in the crib again. Annie covered her with a blanket.

"Rub her back," Annie said. "She likes that."

Josh's big hand splayed across the baby's tiny back, rubbing in a circle. Hannah slipped her thumb into her mouth and closed her eyes. After a few minutes, he pulled his hand away. Hannah didn't stir.

He smiled broadly at Annie. "I think it worked."

"You're a natural," she said. "You can get up with her every night from now on."

Josh turned to Annie beside him, looking pleased with himself. "Any other miracles I can perform tonight?"

She smiled. "Not that I know of."

He stepped a little closer. "Any other females in the house who need their back rubbed?"

It sounded heavenly. Annie summoned all of her strength to shake her head. "No."

"Well, then, I'd better go," Josh said, but made no move to leave the nursery. "You're sure there's nothing else you need?"

He sounded sincere and concerned, which surprised Annie. That she could have easily poured out all her problems to him surprised her, too. Told him everything, knowing he'd find a way to make things better for her.

But to do that would reveal her inadequacies and increase the chance of losing her job…among other things.

"I'll talk to Mrs. Flanders and the rest of the staff, like you asked," Josh said. "I'll see to it that they don't interfere with the children again."

She'd forgotten for a moment that she'd asked him to do that this evening during their argument in his study. It pleased her that Josh had remembered.

And he'd agreed to do it her way. To let her, and her alone, control the children. No more of Mrs. Flanders undermining her authority, regardless of what Annie wanted for the children.

"Thank you," Annie said.

"You're welcome."

They stood together in the dim light, staring into each other's eyes, neither moving.

"I should get into bed," Annie said, stepping back. "And so should you."

Josh's chest expanded as he sucked in a quick breath. Annie's cheeks flamed.

"I didn't mean together—I meant that I should— and that you should, but—"

"It's all right," Josh said softly. "I understand what you meant."

Annie twisted her fingers together, relieved. "Well, good night."

"Good night."

Annie stood rooted to the floor, caught in Josh's

gaze, unable to move. He seemed in no hurry to leave, either.

"Thank you," she said, motioning toward the crib, "for helping with Hannah."

"You're welcome."

They looked at each other for a while longer. Finally, Annie backed away, carrying with her the soft, caring expression on Josh's face.

Chapter Sixteen

When she saw him again the next morning, he looked nothing like she'd remembered from the night before. Striding toward her as she came down the stairs, he stopped in front of her, frowning.

"I did as you asked," he told her. "I told Mrs. Flanders no one but you was to have anything to say about the children."

Annie's stomach twisted. "And?"

"And she quit," Josh told her. "Mrs. Flanders quit."

"She quit?"

"She quit."

"Mrs. Flanders quit? Just like that?"

"Just like that," Josh said.

"But…" Annie shook her head. "I don't understand."

Josh flung out both arms. "Damned if I understand, either."

"She's worked here for years, hasn't she? Since you were married?"

"I guess that's the problem," Josh said, pushing his fingers through his hair. "The best I could gather from her ranting and raving was that she hadn't been happy with how things were going since Lydia died. The children, the nannies, everything. So when I told her she wasn't to interfere with your authority over the children, she—"

"This is my fault." Annie gasped. "Mrs. Flanders quit because of me. Because you did what I asked you to do."

Josh waved his hands again, confused, not sure where blame belonged, if anywhere. "Anyway, she's gone."

"Maybe she was just upset? Maybe she'll come back?"

Josh shrugged. "No. She packed up her things already and left. Said she was going back to Philadelphia. Back to civilization."

"I feel terrible about this," Annie said, touching her hand to her throat.

She watched Josh closely for a sign that he blamed her, or was upset with her, but saw indications of neither. Still, Mrs. Flanders had quit because of her actions. Annie wondered what the rest of the staff would think. And what the rest of the settlement would say when word got out.

"What are you going to do?" Annie asked.

"Nothing," Josh said. "Hell, I'm not even sure what Mrs. Flanders did in the first place."

"A house this size needs someone to make sure

things get done on time, to keep everything running smoothly.''

He waved away Annie's concern, seemingly anxious to put the whole matter behind him. ''We'll be fine.''

''But—''

''I've got work to do.'' Josh walked away.

Annie watched him go, watched him disappear down the hallway and around the corner. For a moment she considered going after him. Obviously, he didn't realize the scope of running a house this size. The servants, the cleaning, the cooking, the supplies all had to be managed properly. Things didn't just get done on their own.

''Mind your own business,'' Annie mumbled.

Josh thought she was a simple girl from a simple background, Angus Martin's poor relation. If she went to Josh and told him her concerns about the running of the house, he'd surely ask her how she knew. And what could she tell him that wouldn't lead to more questions?

Questions Annie didn't want to answer. Couldn't afford to answer.

Annie took one final look down the hall, then went upstairs.

The children had taken to sleeping later, much to Annie's relief. She didn't know if the baby crying at night awakened them and interfered with their sleep, or if they'd simply worn themselves out from rising so early and roaming the farm. Either way,

Annie was glad to find them still in their rooms, only now waking.

"Mrs. Flanders don't live here no more?" Drew asked, rubbing his eyes.

Annie was surprised the children had learned the news so quickly, until she heard Georgia humming in the nursery next door and figured she must have told them.

"That's right," Annie said.

"When are you leaving?" Ginny asked, climbing out of bed.

"I'm not leaving," Annie told her. "I'm here to stay."

Cassie looked up hopefully. "Really? You're not going to leave us?"

"Yes, she is," Ginny said, taking her little sister's hand and leading her to the washstand in the corner. "They all leave."

"Wait just a minute. Drew, come over here." Annie knelt in front of the children, the three of them yawning, rubbing their eyes. "I know you've had a lot of nannies in the past few months, but that's changed now. I'm here to stay. I'm not going to leave you."

They looked at her, gauging her words. Cassie looked hopeful, Drew indifferent and Ginny distrustful.

"Just wait. You'll see." Annie smiled and rose. "All right, now, get dressed and go down for your breakfast. And don't—don't!—leave the house until I get down there."

Annie went into the nursery and found Georgia rocking Hannah, feeding her and smiling from ear to ear.

"From the look on your face I take it you're happy about Mrs. Flanders's departure," Annie said.

Georgia's smile widened. "Best dang news I've heard in a month of Sundays. That ol' Mrs. Flanders harped in my ear from dawn to dusk, and then some. Can't say I'm sorry she's cleared outa' here."

"I think she'd been unhappy here for a while," Annie said. "Since Mrs. Ingalls died."

"Them two was a couple of peas in a pod, that's for sure," Georgia said. "Who you reckon Mr. Ingalls is going to hire to take her place?"

Annie shrugged. "I don't know."

Georgia pressed her lips together thoughtfully. "Probably check into one of them agencies back east again. That's what he's done before."

"I'll take Hannah now so you can get on with your chores," Annie offered.

"If it's all the same to you," Georgia said, smiling down at Hannah, "I'd like to hang on to this little baby a while longer and feed her the rest of her breakfast. Reckon I got me a little free time this morning, seeing as how that Mrs. Flanders ain't jawing in my ear."

"I'll be back up later to check on you two," Annie said, and headed downstairs.

The children were seated in the cookhouse having their breakfast when Annie walked in. Tension hung heavy in the room, along with the smell of bacon and biscuits. Mrs. Royce eased up beside Annie, wringing her apron in her hands.

"Is it true? Is it true what I heard about Mrs. Flanders?" she asked.

Annie nodded. "Yes. She's gone. Left this morning."

"And she didn't even tell us goodbye," Mrs. Royce said, shaking her head sorrowfully. "Well, then, who's taking over?"

"Nobody that I know of," Annie told her.

"Nobody?" Mrs. Royce's eyes widened until her brows nearly touched her hairline. "Nobody? But who's going to order the supplies and plan the meals? What am I supposed to cook?"

Annie resisted the temptation to promise Mrs. Royce that she'd talk to Josh tonight, get things straightened out. But it wasn't her place to do so.

She patted the woman's arm. "I'm sure everything will be worked out in due time."

"Well, I don't know…" Mrs. Royce went back to the stove, shaking her head.

After breakfast, Annie took the children outside under the shade of the trees beside the house and tried to get them to play games together. They'd have no part of it.

"We don't want to play games," Ginny told her.

"Then how about if we build ourselves a tent?" Annie suggested.

"You know how to do that?" Drew asked, wiping his nose on his shirtsleeve.

"Of course," Annie told him. "We can pretend it's a fort, or a store, or a house."

"Yipee!" Cassie bounced on her toes. "Can we bring our dolls outside, too?"

"Sure, we can—"

"We don't want to play in a tent," Ginny said.

Cassie looked up at her. "But, Ginny—"

"We want to play in our room," Ginny said. "By ourselves."

Annie sighed, trying not to let her disappointment show. "Well, all right, if that's what you want. Go on back inside. And don't run in the house."

Ginny turned away, then looked back at Annie. "I heard you and Papa talking about us breaking that statue."

It surprised her to realize that Ginny must have sneaked down the stairs and listened outside Josh's study.

"Ginny, it's not polite to eavesdrop."

"How come you told Papa not to punish us?"

Annie gazed down at her grim little face, a face tight with worries and concerns beyond her years. "Because, Ginny, what happens between us stays between us."

"What does that mean?" Drew asked.

"It means I'm not a tattletale."

Ginny just looked at her for another minute, then led the way into the house. Annie watched them go, sure the children couldn't remain aloof for too much longer. Of course, they were a solid unit. They'd depended on each other—and no one else—for a long time. Annie decided she'd try breaking up that unit.

After the children had played in their room for a while, Annie fetched Cassie and took her away. Ginny and Drew, especially Ginny, weren't happy about it, and Cassie looked a little frightened as Annie led her to the balcony at the back of the house, carrying Hannah on her hip.

"I think it's time Hannah got to know her sister a little better," Annie said, settling them on the old quilt she kept out there.

It took a while, but gradually Cassie warmed up to the idea of spending time with Annie and Hannah. She talked to her little sister, held her hands as she pulled up, and shared her toys. Annie sat both the girls on her lap and read them a story from a book she'd found on the shelves in the children's room.

"My turn," Cassie declared, when Annie had read the first two pages. She took the book from Annie and proceeded to read.

Annie's eyes bulged as she read along with Cassie. The story was simple and the words small, but the child didn't miss a thing.

"Cassie, did you memorize this story?" she asked.

"Nope." She looked up, smiling. "I'm reading. Ginny taught me."

"How old are you?" Annie asked. She'd guessed her age at around four, but wasn't so sure now.

"Almost five. Can I read some more?"

"Sure."

When they finished the story, Annie let Cassie give Hannah her bottle before sending her back to her room with Ginny and Drew.

"I gotta go?" Cassie asked, looking a little disappointed.

"It's time for your sister's nap," Annie explained. "But we can do this again tomorrow, if you'd like?"

"Okay," Cassie said, and smiled at Annie. "I had fun."

"Me, too."

Cassie skipped down the hallway.

A victory. At last. Annie could have leaped for joy. Finally, she'd gotten somewhere with one of the children. Granted, her victory was small, but still, it was a victory. Now it was only a matter of time before Ginny and Drew came around.

How smart she'd thought she was a few days ago, believing she was actually making progress with the children.

How smart, indeed, Annie thought, cleaning up the coffee she'd spilled when she'd discovered a small frog floating in her cup.

In the past few days, the children's behavior had continued to worsen. They found inkwells and drew pictures on their own hands and one of the upstairs walls. They scribbled all over two of their storybooks; Annie was just thankful they hadn't found the scissors.

At church on Sunday, the children raced away as

soon as Josh pulled the surrey into the churchyard, and pretended they didn't hear her when she called to them to leave. When they returned home, Ginny and Drew got into a slapping match leaving the surrey; the only good thing about that was it saved Annie the embarrassment of reliving the Sunday afternoon nap debacle from the first week they'd attended church.

The following day, Drew climbed one of the big oaks that surrounded the house and refused to come down. When Annie tried to climb up after him, he hurled acorns at her. That night, she found mounds of talc in her bureau drawers, dumped there by the children.

The next day they left the house again without permission while Annie was tending to Hannah, and created so much havoc at the barn that the foreman brought them back himself.

Still, through it all, Annie insisted on Cassie spending a few hours every day with her and Hannah on the balcony. And she refused to tell Josh what had happened. She was going to manage those three children—or die trying.

As Annie was going up to bed that evening, it occurred to her that she might really die trying. She was exhausted. Hannah had kept her up most of the night, hadn't wanted to nap, didn't want her bottle, while the oldest three wreaked havoc on everything and everybody—especially Annie.

On top of that, Annie had somehow become the repository for all the servants' complaints. Mrs.

Royce had chased her down wanting to know what to fix for supper, who was going to order supplies and when. One of her two helpers had threatened to quit. Even Georgia and the other two maids were at loose ends, not sure what to do when. The house was showing signs of neglect.

And of course, Josh had hardly been home. Whatever it was he did all day suddenly seemed to take even more of his time. He left before sunrise and returned after sundown. He ate, then went to bed, refusing to speak to any of the servants or address their problems.

Tonight Annie had intended to wait up until Josh got home, and talk to him. Something had to be done about the problems around the house. And he was the only one who could do that.

But it was very late and Annie was very tired. She decided to go to bed, get up early and talk to him in the morning.

As she climbed the stairs, a commotion broke out behind her. She turned and saw Josh striding toward her, surrounded by four of the servants, all of them chattering away. He waved his arms, overwhelmed by the cacophony, then finally stopped still.

"Quiet!"

The women fell silent and drew back as he glared down at them.

"What's wrong?" Annie asked, coming back down the stairs.

"It's that Mr. Douglas," Mrs. Royce began. A roar of voices rose after hers.

"I said quiet!" Josh shouted again.

He turned, pinning Annie with his gaze. "It seems that since Mrs. Flanders is gone, *I* have to do the planning for Douglas's visit."

"You?" Annie asked. "But—"

Josh pointed his finger at Annie. "And *you're* going to help me."

Chapter Seventeen

"Sit." Josh pointed to the chair across from his desk, grabbing a handful of papers.

Annie stood her ground, refusing to sit. "I can't help you with this party, I'm already busy with the children."

"I sure as hell don't know anything about it!"

"Really, it's not such a big problem," Annie told him. "Nothing you can't handle."

"Forty people! Mrs. Flanders invited forty people!"

She blanched. "Forty?"

"Yes!"

Josh heaved the papers he'd gathered onto the floor. He was tired from working all day, and he was hungry. He'd walked into the cookhouse tonight expecting his supper, only to be pounced on by Mrs. Royce and her two helpers the minute he set his foot through the door, the three of them squawking and wringing their hands about everything under the sun.

They were out of supplies, they needed this, they needed that. Who would order them? How would they pay for them? What were they going to do about the meals, the menus?

Then the maids had joined in, making demands, wanting to know what and when to clean. He'd been surrounded. Ambushed.

He'd almost gotten away from them when Mrs. Royce suddenly announced that forty people were coming for Thomas Douglas's reception and nothing had been prepared. For an instant, he'd thought the woman might actually faint.

"Forty? Oh, dear..." Annie eased into the chair across from his desk.

Trying to calm himself, Josh drew in a big breath and plowed his fingers through his hair. He winced and shook his left hand. He'd busted his knuckles working today and they stung.

"You've hurt yourself," Annie said, rising from the chair again. "Let me see."

"It's nothing," he grumbled.

"No, let me see," she insisted, and rounded the desk.

Annoyed, Josh stood his ground, refusing to move aside as Annie squeezed next to him. Not that his hand didn't hurt. Not that it didn't need attention.

But he didn't want it from Annie.

For days he'd deliberately stayed away from the house—in order to stay away from her. He'd gotten up early and left; he'd stayed away until late. He'd gone straight to bed, all to avoid spending time with Annie.

Now here she was, holding his hand, looking fresh and sweet and smelling good, standing right under his nose. How much could a man take?

He'd thought about her. Even when he'd been working like a dog these past days, Annie hadn't been far from his thoughts.

He'd tried to shut her out. Tried to shut out a lot of things. But couldn't.

"Come to the cookhouse," Annie said, patting his hand gently. "This needs to be cleaned."

She walked away, not bothering to look back, knowing, somehow, that he would follow.

And he did. Like a jackass on a lead rope, Josh trailed Annie down the hallway, mesmerized by her long legs and swaying hips.

The cookhouse was empty, Mrs. Royce and her two helpers gone, probably plotting their resignations, the way his luck had run lately.

Annie lit the lantern and found a basin in the cupboards—not without an undue amount of bending and stretching, much to Josh's distress. She pumped water into it, fetched a clean towel, found the little chest of medical supplies and reached for his hand.

Lord help him, he thought he'd grab her right there. Haul her up on the worktable and spend a few pleasurable hours satisfying the desperate urges that had claimed him. If she touched him—even his hand—he couldn't be held responsible for his actions.

But when Annie took his hand, everything changed.

A calm coursed through Josh that he couldn't remember ever experiencing before. As if every problem he had, or ever might have, simply dissolved at her touch.

He hardly noticed as she cleaned his hand, plucked out a splinter or two. All he could focus on was Annie. Her gentle touch. The care with which she tended to him. The way she smelled.

Somehow, nothing seemed like a huge dilemma anymore. Not even the party he had to see to. With Annie at his side, everything seemed just fine.

"There you go, good as new," Annie said, dabbing the scrape dry. "You should watch it, though, in case it festers."

Josh glanced down at his hand and moved a little closer to her. But she stepped away just as quickly.

"You must be hungry," Annie said. She nodded toward the table. "Sit down. I'll find you something to eat."

He didn't sit down, just stood where he was, even though he was in her way and she had to step around him. She didn't seem to mind, and he sure as hell didn't.

After she warmed up the chicken and potatoes left from supper, and poured him a cup of coffee, Annie sat with him at the table while he ate.

"How did your work go today?" she asked.

"Got a lot done," he said between bites of food.

"Putting up new fencing and building a feeder shed. How about you?"

"Fine," she said, and gave him a quick smile. "Everything was just fine here at the house today."

She was lying. Annie didn't have much of a poker face and he could read it easily, so he knew she hadn't told him the truth. Plus he knew his own children.

Still, he appreciated that Annie wanted to handle her job herself. That was a quality he admired in people, Annie in particular.

He appreciated, too, that she didn't barrage him with a litany of her woes and his children's antics, as most of the other nannies had done. She'd kept that burden off his shoulders by putting it squarely on her own.

They made small talk in the quiet kitchen until he'd finished eating. Annie took his plate away, brought him more coffee and a cup for herself.

"So, about this party," Josh said, looking pointedly across the table at her.

"Yes?" she asked, being deliberately evasive.

Josh grunted. "I'm not sure where to start. We'll have to feed these people, but Mrs. Royce claims she doesn't know what to serve."

"Surely you've had parties before," Annie said. "Before, when your wife was here?"

"Hell…" He sipped his coffee. "Lydia had the house full of people all the time."

"Can't Mrs. Royce prepare something? She must know what to do."

"She says that Lydia and Mrs. Flanders gave her specific instructions on everything," Josh said. "And, she doesn't have any of the recipes."

Annie looked around the cookhouse. "There must be dozens of recipes here, somewhere."

"But where? That's the issue," Josh said. "Mrs. Flanders kept them in her possession, and probably took them with her when she left. And if they're still in the house, who knows where she stored them?"

Annie sat back and lifted her shoulders in resignation. "You'll have to ask Mrs. Baird for help. Next to you, her family is the wealthiest in the settlement. She'll know what to do—"

"Like hell." Josh sat back and dragged his hand down his face. "The last thing I want is Eleanor Baird sticking her nose in over here, bringing that daughter of hers with her."

"What other choice do you have?" Annie asked.

"You can help me."

Annie shook her head. "No, I can't."

"Yes, you can."

"Why me?"

"Because there is nobody else." Josh pushed his coffee cup aside. "Look, Annie, I know you have your hands full with the children. But I've got a lot to do for planting season. I can't waste time planning a party."

"But—"

"Just do the best you can," Josh said. "I realize your circumstances—"

Her back stiffened. "My circumstances?"

"Yes, your background," he said. "I don't expect much, and neither will any of the guests. Everyone will understand."

"I see." Annie's cheeks flushed as she rose from the chair.

Her lips trembled slightly, and for an instant Josh thought she might cry. Then her expression hardened.

"No, Mr. Ingalls, I can't help you."

Annie walked out of the cookhouse.

She dashed up the stairs and into her room, closing the door behind her, trying to hold on to her anger. If she let it slip, she'd surely cry.

Not much made her cry anymore. But this might.

It hadn't occurred to Josh that Annie, or her family, knew how to put on a proper party, how to entertain guests. He assumed she didn't. Assumed her and her family to be the poor relations of Angus Martin. People of little consequence.

Dropping to her knees in front of the open window, Annie gazed out at the night sky. She sniffed. Tears pressed against her eyes.

Of course, why wouldn't Josh assume her poor? She'd told him how her family had moved from relative to relative these past few years, seeking anyone kind enough to take them in.

And look how she dressed.

Annie gazed down at her faded trousers and her

shirt with the mismatched buttons. She'd always felt so comfortable in them, but now...

Before, the manner in which her family was forced to live had been all right with her. After her father's death, she, her mother and her sisters had put their previous life in St. Louis behind them and gone on as best they could. It had been painfully hard on their mother. Difficult, too, for her sisters— Willa in particular. But it had never bothered Annie. Until now.

And now, for some reason, she wanted Josh to think highly of her. She didn't want him looking down on her, thinking ill of her and her family.

Annie gulped back the lump in her throat. At least he hadn't heard about her sister.

And that's why she hadn't told him the truth when he asked her to help plan the party. If she'd told him the truth about her family's background, about how easily she could have managed the party preparations, he'd have started asking questions. She'd have opened the door and invited him into her past. Then there would have been no stopping him.

Sooner or later, Josh would find out about Willa's pregnancy. Then he would fire Annie. He certainly couldn't have his children tended to by a nanny whose family's morals were the talk of the settlement.

So she'd refused to help with the party, when, in fact, she would have loved to do it. Annie closed her eyes, imagining the beautiful Ingalls home decorated with fresh flowers, the grand dining room table laden with silver trays of delicious foods, men in cravats and women in beautiful gowns.

Herself in a beautiful gown.

Annie let the fantasy play out in her mind, indulging in the vision of her entering the parlor wearing a breathtaking gown, catching the eye of every man in the room.

No, Annie decided. Not every man in the room. One man. Just one.

Josh.

Annie folded her hands on the windowsill and sighed heavily. Could she tell him the truth about her sister, her family? If she did, would he understand?

For a moment she envisioned doing just that. She could go down to the cookhouse right now and find Josh, divulge everything. Trust that he wouldn't turn against her. She could do that, confess all, get everything off her chest, relieve herself of the burden of deception she'd carried with her. Josh would understand, wouldn't he?

Maybe. Annie sat back. Yes, he might understand. But what if he didn't? What if he turned against her?

Annie squeezed her eyes closed. She'd never bear up under his scorn. Her cousin's, yes. She could handle that. Even the settlement's. But not Josh's.

She couldn't take the chance. Because if he didn't

accept her as she was, if he fired her, what would become of her family? They needed her.

She wouldn't let them down.

Not even for Josh.

A little tear rolled down Annie cheek. No, not even for Josh.

Chapter Eighteen

It was no use.

At noon, Josh tied his horse to the post at the back of his house and went inside, dragging his shirt-sleeve across his sweaty forehead. It was no use. He couldn't stay away. Not anymore. Not after last night.

Being alone with Annie in the cookhouse had been special, even if she had gotten up abruptly and left. He'd thought about it all morning when he should have been working, and finally decided he must have hurt her feelings, asking her to help with planning the party when she had no idea what to do. It was thoughtless of him, really. Annie had her pride and he'd squashed it good. He'd have to figure some way to make it up to her.

When he walked into the cookhouse, Mrs. Royce turned on him, no doubt ready to unleash another geyser of problems. Josh held up his hand, warning her off, then went into the bathing room and washed.

"I'll be down later to eat," he told her on his way back through, then took the steps upstairs.

Josh had seen no sign of the children outside this morning, and now heard nothing of them up here, either. Disappointed, he checked in their room. Empty. What he really wanted to do was talk to Annie.

As an afterthought, he checked the back balcony. His heart rate picked up a bit when he saw her seated in the rocker. But as he walked outside, he saw it wasn't Annie, but a younger version of her.

"Camille?"

She looked up from the book on her lap and smiled shyly. "Hello, Mr. Ingalls. I hope it's all right that I'm here. Annie said you gave your permission for me to study some of your books."

He nodded. How could he forget selecting the books for her, when he'd ended up kissing Annie?

"You're going away to school?"

"Oh, yes," Camille said, clutching the book against her and smiling dreamily. "The Hayden Academy for Young Women."

Josh couldn't help smiling at her enthusiasm. "Is it a good school?"

"The best," Camille told him. "They teach history and literature and mathematics. Annie picked it out and made all the arrangements."

"Annie did?" he asked, mildly surprised that she, not their mother, had taken on that responsibility. "Where is this school?"

"Richmond."

"Virginia? That's a long way from home."

"That's what Annie wanted," Camille said, nodding earnestly. "She says it's best I'm as far away from the scand—"

Camille gasped and slumped back in her chair, clutching her book tighter as her cheeks pinkened. She gulped. "That is, well, Annie said it's best that I—I go to the finest school I can, no matter where it is."

Poor lying skills ran in the Martin family, it seemed. Josh changed the subject. "Where's Annie?"

"She took the children for a walk," Camille said, looking relieved by this different topic of conversation. "They left just a few minutes ago, so I don't expect them back for a while."

Josh grunted. "I wanted to talk to Annie about the party preparations."

Camille's face lit up. "Annie is helping plan the party? Oh, she's so good at these things. Mama taught her."

"Is that so?"

"Oh, yes. Papa died a long time ago, but I still remember the parties, sneaking out of my bed at night watching the ladies in their gowns, hearing the music. I couldn't wait until I got old enough to attend."

"Then you'll have to come to this party," Josh said.

Camille sprang to the edge of her chair. "Could

I? Really? Oh, how wonderful. Thank you so much. You're sure it's all right?''

''I'm sure.''

''Thank you.'' Camille smiled broadly. ''And thank you for letting me study your books.''

''You're welcome.''

Josh left the balcony and headed back downstairs frowning and rubbing his chin. Annie had led him to believe she didn't know anything about planning a party, but obviously she did. And why was she sending her sister all the way to Virginia for schooling?

Maybe he should ask her.

Georgia waited in the hallway as Annie tucked the children into bed for the night and turned down the wall lantern. She was glad for an adult to talk to. The children had worn her out today.

Despite their protests, Annie had insisted they all take a walk together. She'd talked to them, gotten a few grumbled responses, and even gotten them involved in a game of tag. Cassie was the most cooperative. Drew was doing a little better, opening up to her some.

Or so she'd thought until they stopped to rest and eat the cookies she'd brought along, and Drew dropped a grasshopper down her shirt.

She'd dismissed it as a childish prank until supper tonight, when she'd sat down in a plateful of potatoes the children had left in her chair.

Annie had admonished them not to do it again,

but they'd paid her little attention. For a moment, she considered going to Josh, asking for his advice and his help. After all, they were his children. Maybe he could offer some insight.

But in the end, Annie had kept it to herself, thinking it wiser not to make too much of the pranks. Doing so would only encourage them. It would also demonstrate to Josh that she couldn't do her job.

"Mr. Ingalls wants to talk to you," Georgia said as Annie walked into the hallway.

She paused. The last time Georgia had sought her out Josh had been upset with her over the children's behavior. They'd ended up in a terrible argument.

"Did he look upset?" Annie asked.

"Naw." Georgia shook her head. "But if he had good sense, he would be. Not 'cause of you, you understand. Mostly 'cause of what's been going on around this place since Mrs. Flanders left. Or rather, what ain't been going on, if you get my meaning."

Annie nodded. She knew exactly what Georgia meant. Without Mrs. Flanders to direct and supervise the staff, little was getting done. And Thomas Douglas was expected to arrive in only a few days.

"Maybe you ought to talk to Mr. Ingalls?" Georgia suggested.

"Me?" The last thing she wanted was to butt into Josh's business—again.

"Mostly 'cause he'll listen to you. Whenever he sees one of us coming at him, he turns tail and heads out." Georgia flapped her hands at her side. "Lordy me, I'm 'fraid that Mr. Douglas fella is going to show up and have to cook his own supper.''

"All right," Annie said. "I'll talk to Mr. Ingalls and see what I can do."

When she got downstairs, she found Josh seated behind his desk in his study. Seeing him like this, bathed in the warm lamplight, never failed to make Annie's heart skip a beat. Tonight was no exception.

She lingered in the doorway for a moment, soaking up the sight of him, then went inside before he looked up and caught her staring.

"Georgia said you wanted to see me?" She took a seat in the chair she always used across the desk from him.

He didn't seem upset or mad, as she'd feared when Georgia gave her the message to come down here. Instead, he looked calmer than she'd seen him lately.

Annie could have sat there all night looking at him—upset or not.

He held up a dog-eared, stained book. "I found the recipes."

She smiled. "Wonderful. I guess Mr. Douglas's party is saved."

"Maybe not," he cautioned, "since I'm the one deciding on what to serve."

He pushed the book across the desk toward her. "Look at this one, will you? Tell me what you think?"

Annie eyed the book cautiously. "Why ask me?"

"Because you're a woman," he told her with a

little grin. "Don't try and deny it. I know it to be a fact. And as a woman, you should have an opinion on this sort of thing."

"Because I'm a woman?" She raised her brows. "I should just *know* this?"

He tilted his head. "Unless there's some other reason you would know what to serve at a party."

He'd said it quite innocently, but Annie had known Josh long enough to suspect something else was behind his casual remark.

"Such as?" she asked, refusing to give anything away.

He shrugged nonchalantly. "Such as you're a European princess living in exile, accustomed to giving lavish parties?"

Annie laughed softly. "No."

He waited, as if expecting her to say more. When she didn't, Josh sat back in his chair.

"Your sister was here today," he said.

Annie tensed. "I know. You said she could come over and read some of your books."

"She told me all about this school you've arranged for her to attend. Seemed anxious to go, even if it is all the way to Virginia." Josh looked across the desk at her. "That's a long way from home. Why did you pick one so far away?"

"Because it's an excellent school."

"Yes, it may be, but—"

"Speaking of school," Annie said. "Did you know Cassie can already read?"

Josh shrugged. "No, can't say as I did."

"Well, she can. And rather well, too. I was wondering what you thought about her starting school when the other children go back?"

He lifted his shoulders. "Sounds fine to me."

"Perhaps you should speak with the teacher first? See what she thinks?" Annie suggested. "Cassie is a bit young, but there's no point holding her back, since she's reading already. She might prefer being with her brother and sister, or perhaps it would be better if she wasn't."

Josh rubbed the back of his neck. "Those are a lot of really good questions."

"Oh, and before I forget to mention it, when Mr. Douglas is gone and things settle down again, I think it would be a good idea if you'd spend some time with the children individually. Especially Drew. He needs a man's influence."

Josh blew out a heavy breath and his shoulders slumped a little.

"Sorry." Annie managed an apologetic smile. She'd overwhelmed him, but that was her intention. Anything to change the subject. "I suppose you miss your wife at times like this."

She expected him to agree, but instead Josh bristled and started sorting through the papers on his desk.

"I have work to finish up," he said, not looking at her. "Good night."

"I've upset you."

"No—"

"Yes, I have," Annie said. "I'm sorry. I won't mention your wife again."

"No, it's not that."

"Then what is it?" she asked.

"It's nothing."

"It's something."

Josh shifted in his chair and rubbed his palms together, working up to explain. "*We* didn't decide things concerning the children," he finally said. "*She* did."

Annie just stared at him.

"The children, the house, the staff—they were Lydia's responsibility," Josh explained. "I took care of everything else."

"You had no say in the upbringing of any of your own children?"

Josh took a breath. "That's what Lydia wanted."

"And that was all right with you?" Annie asked, unable to keep the shock out of her voice.

"That's what Lydia wanted," he told her with a finality that ended the conversation.

No wonder Josh hardly knew his children. No wonder he spent no time with them. All along she'd been thinking it was his wish, his choice. Now she knew it was neither.

"Well, then, good night," Annie said, rising from the chair.

Josh turned back to his work without answering. Annie waited a few seconds, wondering if he'd mention the menu again. When he didn't, she left. As she climbed the stairs she heard his footsteps in the hallway below, then the front door close with a thud.

Not for the first time, Annie wanted to go after him. She didn't know what she'd say or do, but she wanted to comfort him somehow.

But she didn't dare.

Chapter Nineteen

The next morning the household was in near chaos. Mr. Douglas was expected to arrive anyday now and nothing was ready. Josh was gone, as usual, leaving Annie the focal point for the staff's distress.

"Didn't Mr. Ingalls pick out menus last night?" Annie asked to Mrs. Royce as they stood together in the cookhouse.

"He did, but they're wrong. All wrong," she said, twisting her apron in her hands. "Mrs. Ingalls would never have served such things to her guests. Never in a hundred years."

Annie sighed. Maybe she should have helped Josh last night when he'd asked her. "Whatever he picked out I'm sure will be fine," she said, trying to sound reasonable and consoling.

"But I can't cook it." Mrs. Royce flung both arms into the air, flapping as if she were trying to take flight. "It doesn't match up with all the supplies Mrs. Flanders already bought and had delivered."

Annie pressed her lips together. She really had no choice now but to solve this problem.

"All right, Mrs. Royce, I'll talk to Mr. Ingalls tonight and see—"

"But that's too late. Some of these things might need preparation right away. I can't wait," she declared. "And on top of that, I still haven't been told what I'm supposed to be making for this party come Saturday night."

Georgia came into the cookhouse just then.

"Me and the other girls can't work like this," she told Annie. "Mrs. Flanders always told us what we're supposed to do first, what to do next, what to do after that. We don't know which way to turn without her. We're all of us just bickering among ourselves, trying to decide on something."

"One of my girls threatened to quit already," Mrs. Royce said.

Annie cringed. If that happened, there was no way a party for forty guests could be prepared.

She could only imagine how Josh would react, faced with that possibility.

"All right, fine. I'll handle everything," Annie promised. "By this afternoon, I'll have answers to all your questions. Everything will be taken care of in plenty of time."

Annie considered getting a horse from the barn, riding out, finding Josh and insisting he come home and help with these problems. However, she feared having Josh here would only add to the confusion.

And, really, she wanted to help him. Since she'd

first set foot on the Ingalls farm, Annie had struggled
to mind her own business. If ever Josh needed her,
it was now.

Yet nosing in this time might reveal more of her
past than she wanted Josh to know, which might
result in her losing her job.

"I'll help under one condition," Annie announced. Both Georgia and Mrs. Royce gave her
their full attention. "I want you both to promise you
won't tell Mr. Ingalls what I've done."

"Shoot, Annie, he'd be tickled pink knowing you
helped out," Georgia said.

"I think the same," Mrs. Royce said.

"I'm supposed to be taking care of the children,"
Annie explained. "I don't want him to think I've
neglected them and stuck my nose in where it
doesn't belong."

Both women understood her reasoning. They nodded in agreement.

"Come upstairs with me," Annie said to Georgia.
"We'll pick out a room for Mr. Douglas to use."

The doors in the long upstairs hallway always remained closed, except for the bedrooms she, Josh
and the children used.

"Are these other rooms all bedrooms?" Annie
asked.

When Georgia nodded, Annie opened the door at
the end of the hall. The room was sparsely furnished, the bed stripped bare.

"I think we can do better than this for Mr. Douglas," Annie said, moving on.

When she got to the next room, Georgia stopped her.

"Oh, no, Annie, you can't be giving that room to Mr. Douglas, or anybody else, for that matter."

She paused with her hand on the knob. "Why not?"

Georgia looked at her as if she'd taken leave of her senses. "'Cause that's Miss Lydia's room."

Annie stepped back and looked at the door, then at the door to Josh's room down the hall. "Lydia's room?"

Georgia nodded.

"Her bedroom?"

"Yep."

"Where she…slept?"

Georgia eyed the distance between this room and Josh's. She sighed longingly. "Like I told you. A man like him? What a waste."

"Oh, dear…"

"Yep. A damn waste."

They inspected the rest of the bedrooms and finally decided Mr. Douglas should occupy the one at the end of the hall, the farthest from the children's rooms. Annie wrote out a list of things to do to ready the room, then made another list of chores to prepare the rest of the house.

"Get the other girls started on these things," Annie said, presenting the lists to Georgia. "When it's done, we'll see what else needs attention. Let me know if you have any problems."

"Sure thing," Georgia said, tucking the lists in her apron pocket.

Annie spent the next hour in the cookhouse, with Hannah on her hip drooling on her shoulder, while she and Mrs. Royce made a list of all the provisions Mrs. Flanders had purchased from Kelsey's Mercantile, as well as those already on-hand. Once Annie had a firm idea what was available, she could begin on the menus.

With so much to accomplish, Annie thought, the children would pick this day to be at their worst. Hannah, getting another tooth, fussed and whined continually. She napped only briefly. The older children wouldn't go outside, even after Annie suggested it. They ran through the house, slid down the staircase using a rug for a sleigh, and banged on the piano in the parlor. When Annie finally got the menus to Mrs. Royce, the papers were crumbled and milk stained, and one corner was ripped off.

As soon as they finished their supper, Annie sent the children upstairs to bed. Her head was hurting, as were her arms from carrying Hannah all day. After she tucked in the older children, she gave the baby her bottle and rocked her to sleep.

For a few minutes, Annie stood by the crib making sure Hannah was sleeping soundly. When she didn't stir, Annie stepped into the children's room. In the faint lantern light she saw them tucked into bed, asleep.

Thank goodness, Annie thought, going into her room. The children's behavior had worsened even more lately. Before, they'd ignored her, treated her as if she didn't exist. Now they'd turned their mischief on her. Annie wasn't sure what this meant. Was she making progress? Or losing ground?

At any rate, she was sure it was some sort of test. How far could they push her before she told their father? Before she threw up her hands and quit?

Annie rubbed her fingertips against her temples, anxious to go to bed. Instead, she decided that what she needed was a hot bath. After today, she deserved it. She gathered her things and went downstairs.

The house was silent. There was no sign of the kitchen workers as she passed through the cookhouse to the bathing room. Good. Annie wanted the place to herself. She needed peace and quiet.

She took time to heat the water, filled the tub and added some lavender toilet water she found in the cupboard. In the glow of the lamplight, Annie undressed and slipped into the tub.

Heaven. She sank into the water, letting its warmth close over her head, then came up and leaned back against the tub. She closed her eyes.

Josh came into her mind. Josh, still out in his fields working, she guessed.

When he woke in the morning and found the house running smoothly, would he notice? Would he be pleased?

She thought so. She'd wanted to help him, and she'd done it. Annie just hoped he wouldn't find out she'd had a hand in the running of the household, and that her good intentions wouldn't come back to haunt her.

Gradually, Annie relaxed as the heat of the water soaked into her tired muscles. The day's problems melted away. She closed her eyes.

A noise roused her. Annie sat up, realizing she'd fallen asleep. She blinked and rubbed her eyes but saw no one. The room was empty. She sighed, deciding it must have been her imagination, or perhaps a dream.

Annie hoisted herself out of the tub. She must have slept awhile because the water had cooled. Night air drifted in through the window, chilling her further.

She grabbed the towel, then stopped abruptly. Her clothes. Where were her clothes? Her gaze bounced around the room.

She'd brought her night rail and wrapper downstairs with her and left them on the chair with her towel. But they were gone. Where could they have—

The children.

Annie's temper blossomed. Those children. This was just the sort of prank they would pull. They hadn't been sleeping at all when she'd left them upstairs. They'd sneaked down here and taken her clothes. Who else would have?

Annie threw the towel around her, yanked a knot in it between her breasts and charged out of the bathing room.

"Darn their little hides, I'm going to—oh!"

Josh.

Annie gasped, hopped back inside the bathing room and slammed the door.

Josh. Good gracious, Josh was in the cookhouse. She'd seen him in profile, standing at the worktable, eating. Had he heard her? Had he glimpsed her from the corner of his eye, wringing wet and clad in a towel?

Annie gulped and wrapped her arms across her middle, pressing the towel around her. Seconds dragged by, turning into minutes. She leaned closer to the door, listening. No footsteps. No voices.

Maybe he hadn't seen her. Maybe, if she waited long enough, he would finish his meal and go upstairs. Then she could slip out of the room and—

"Annie?"

She froze. Her body tingled from head to toe. Here she stood stark naked—except for a towel—with Josh only a few feet away on the other side of the door.

What should she do? Answer him? Pretend she wasn't in here?

"Annie, are you all right?"

He sounded concerned, and obviously, he knew she was in here. Her stomach tightened.

"Annie, is something wrong?" Josh's voice through the door sounded slightly irritated now. "Annie?"

"No, nothing is—" Her voice broke. She cleared her throat and tried again. "Nothing is wrong. I'm just…bathing."

"When you're finished I want to talk to you," he said. "I'll wait in the cookhouse."

"No!"

"Excuse me?"

"I mean, no, I can't talk with you in the cookhouse. Why don't you go to your study and I'll meet you there?" That way she could run up the back steps to her room, get dressed and meet him in the study.

"Because I'm eating," he said, sounding a bit annoyed. "I have something to discuss with you. It's important."

"Can't it wait until the morning?"

"I just said it's important," Josh said. "Come out here."

Annie pushed the long strands of her wet hair back off her shoulder. She was cold and getting colder by the minute. She couldn't stand in here all night arguing with him through the closed door.

"I can't come out…right now."

"Why not?"

Annie pressed her lips together. It was bad enough she had to tell him she was stranded without clothes, but to tell him that his children had stolen them from her would only add to her humiliation— and possibly get her fired.

"Well, you see, I forgot to bring clothes down with me," she said.

A long moment dragged by before Josh spoke again. "So, you're…naked?"

"Well…yes."

No sound came from the other side of the door. Was Josh silently laughing at her? Had he gone to fetch her a wrapper? Had he pressed his eye to the keyhole?

Annie stepped aside.

"Except," she said, "I have a towel."

Still she heard nothing. Annie leaned closer to the door, listening. Was that heavy breathing she heard? Or her imagination?

"Josh? Josh, are you there?"

"I'm here." His voice sounded gruff, hoarse, closer to the door.

"I need to go upstairs," Annie said. "I'm cold."

"All right."

"You'll leave?"

"Yes."

"You promise?"

"Yes."

"You won't look?"

"I won't look."

Annie waited another moment, then opened the door a crack. No sign of Josh. Thank goodness.

She hurried out of the room, clutching the towel together, then stopped in her tracks.

Josh stood at the worktable, facing her, grasping the edge as if he might fall over. Annie's first reaction was to run away. But the expression on Josh's face held her in place.

"You're looking."

"You're beautiful."

He said it as if he'd just realized it. As if she were

the first woman in the world he'd ever thought beautiful.

"You're absolutely...beautiful," he breathed.

And, suddenly, Annie didn't want to run away at all. Her gaze met his. He pulled her in, held her captive from across the room.

Annie's body warmed. She'd never been called beautiful before, never had a man look at her as Josh looked at her now. The way a man looks at a woman.

His gaze dipped to her bare feet, followed the long line of her legs to where the towel parted at her thigh, then jumped to her bosom straining over the top of the fabric, and finally to her wet hair hanging over her shoulders.

He came forward slowly, never taking his eyes off of her. Annie didn't back away. Here was where she belonged. In this moment with Josh. Feeling, for the first time in her life, like a woman.

He stopped inches in front of her, his face tense, his mouth set. Surely he'd kiss her. She knew he would. He'd looked that way before, in the field, in his study.

"You're cold?" he asked, his voice barely above a whisper.

With her heart thudding in her chest, Annie nodded, wondering what would happen.

He didn't kiss her, though. Instead, he pulled off his suspenders and slowly opened the buttons of his shirt, all the while watching her.

Annie's heart pounded harder, her knees weakening as Josh shrugged out of his shirt. His long johns stood open to the center of his chest. Dark, crinkly hair curled out like a warm blanket. She'd never wanted to touch a man's chest before in her life. She wanted to now.

Time seemed to stop as Annie gazed into his eyes, and he into hers. Nothing existed but the two of them. And that was fine with Annie.

Josh offered her his shirt. He slipped it on one of her arms, then the other, and pulled the fabric closed in front just below her chin.

Faint disappointment rippled through Annie. That was it? That was all? He'd give her his shirt and send her on her way?

Annie swallowed the knot of emotion that rose in her throat. Of course that was all. Why should she expect more?

Why did she want more?

The answer to her question crept into her mind, startling her, then fled as Josh leaned closer. He claimed her with one arm around her shoulders, then lowered his head and kissed her.

His hot lips covered hers, blending them together, then pushed deep inside her. Annie's head spun as she felt his fingers beneath the shirt, fumbling with the knot between her breasts. He ripped the towel off her and sent it flying across the room.

Josh grasped her bottom and pulled her against him. She gasped at the heat, the hardness of him. Her mind whirled as he kissed her mouth, then dipped his lips to her throat, her shoulder. He pulled back the fabric of the shirt and cradled her breast in his palm, then lowered his head.

With a moan, Annie dug her fingers into his hair. His hands slid downward over the curve of her hip, to her bottom, and back to her breast again when he kissed her greedily. Annie arched backward, sliding her leg along his, splaying her hand across his chest.

Josh groaned as he captured her lips again. His mouth was hot and full on hers, robbing her of all conscious thought, all strength, all will. Annie wanted to be nowhere but here.

A thread of reason curled through her mind. *Here* was the middle of the cookhouse.

She pulled her lips from his. "Josh—"

He tightened his arms around her and buried his mouth against her neck.

"Josh…" Annie pushed on his shoulder. Hard, tight muscles. She didn't budge him. "Josh…the servants might walk in."

He kissed his way up her jaw to her mouth. Annie turned her head. "Josh…the children…"

He stopped, his lips hovering above hers. Hot breath puffed against her mouth.

"The children, they might walk in and…see us," Annie whispered.

Josh groaned softly and eased back, loosening his hold on her. He swallowed hard.

Cool air swirled between them. Annie pulled the shirt closed in front of her and folded her arms together.

"I'd—I'd better go," she said, though she wasn't sure she meant it.

Annie took a step back, then another and another. Josh's gaze burned into her. His body, hard and taut, beckoned her. He didn't call her back or make a move to stop her. He knew she was right.

Annie hurried out of the cookhouse and up the back staircase. At the top she paused, wondering if she'd hear Josh's steps behind her. She didn't. She glanced back. Nothing.

In her room, Annie caught a glimpse of herself in the mirror above the bureau. Her skin was pink, her cheeks flushed.

She should have been embarrassed by her wanton behavior, but wasn't. Being with Josh—touching him, kissing him, having him do the same to her—seemed natural. It seemed right.

The image of her and Josh and a Sunday afternoon together blazed through her mind.

Yet it wasn't right. It wasn't proper.

So why had she allowed it to happen?

A tear trickled from Annie's eye. She sniffed the fabric of Josh's shirt and rubbed it against her cheek, knowing the answer full well.

She'd fallen in love with him.

Chapter Twenty

"All right, now, let's have it. Tell me what's wrong, Annie."

"Oh, Mama." Annie plopped down in the rocker on the back balcony beside her mother. "How did you know?"

"Camille told me," Sophia said, rocking gently with Hannah sleeping in her arms. "Your sister told me that you were upset. What is it, Annie? What's wrong?"

Annie gazed out over the farm, wondering where to start her explanation, or if she should even explain at all. Her mother had strung together quite a few "good" days lately, according to Camille. Would hearing Annie's problem send her back to her bed? Would knowing how her daughter had almost given herself to her employer a few nights ago in the cookhouse cause a relapse?

Probably.

"It's the children," Annie said. She glanced over

her shoulder, down the hallway to their room. They were—supposedly—in there playing. Goodness knows, they could have sneaked out to wreak havoc somewhere on the farm.

"What are they doing?" Sophia asked.

"What *aren't* they doing?" Annie echoed. "At first, it was just mischief in general. Lately, it's been directed at me, personally. Last night I opened my bureau drawer and three crickets hopped out. It's one thing after another with those children."

Sophia smiled. "Pranks. All children go through that phase."

"That's what I thought," Annie said. "But things are escalating. They're getting worse. I don't seem to be reaching them, as I thought I could. I wanted to be friends with them, help them, but now…"

Sophia looked up sharply. "Annie, are you growing more fond of the children than you should?"

Annie couldn't answer. She'd grown more fond of all the Ingalls—especially their father—than she should have.

"You're only their nanny," Sophia said. "You have to keep some distance."

"Yes, I know that, but it's hard not to care about them." Annie smiled and nodded toward Hannah. "Especially her. She's such a dear."

"Indeed she is," Sophia murmured, gazing down at the baby. "It would be hard not to fall in love."

"So what should I do about the older children?" Annie asked. "They don't take me seriously because they think I'll leave, like all the other nannies did."

"Couldn't Mr. Ingalls assure them you're not leaving? That you're going to stay here permanently?"

Annie glanced away. She couldn't go to Josh with such a request. After the night in the cookhouse, he might think it better if she did leave.

Not that she knew for sure, of course. She'd avoided Josh. Which had been easy, because he seemed to be avoiding her, as well.

What does a woman say to a man after such a moment? How could they look at each other and not remember? Not be embarrassed?

Not want to do it again?

"Annie?"

She shifted in her chair, glad for the distraction her mother provided. Dwelling on thoughts of Josh would do no good.

"Maybe I'll talk to Mr. Ingalls about the children," Annie said, though she doubted she'd actually do that.

Sophia nodded and changed the subject. "When is this guest arriving? The whole settlement is talking about him, and the big party."

"He's expected anytime now."

"And who is he?" Sophia asked.

"A Mr. Douglas. From Missouri. He's invented a combination harvester Mr. Ingalls is interested in."

"Mr. Douglas...?" Sophia gazed away for a moment.

"Do you know him?"

Sophia shook her head quickly. "No, I'm sure I don't. Is everything ready for his arrival?"

"It's been difficult with Mrs. Flanders gone, but I believe I've seen to everything. Will you take a walk through the house before you leave today, just to make sure I haven't overlooked anything?"

"Of course," Sophia said. "I'm glad to help out, even if I won't be at the party. I explained it to Camille. She's disappointed that she can't come, of course, but she understands."

Annie knew it hurt her mother that Mrs. Flanders hadn't included her on the guest list. The scandal swirling around Willa made it awkward for Sophia to go anywhere in the settlement, and almost impossible to receive invitations to any of the social functions.

"I can ask Mr. Ingalls," Annie offered. "I'm sure he'll say it's all right for you two to come."

"It will only get people talking—worse than they already are," Sophia said. "Better to leave things be."

"Any word from Evan Keller or his family?"

Sophia shook her head. "Nothing. I wrote them again, but haven't heard. Really, I don't expect that I will, considering everything."

"How is Willa holding up?"

"About the same," Sophia said.

Annie touched her mother's arm. "I know how hard this is for you."

Sophia squeezed Annie's hand. "It's hard on all of us."

"But we'll manage."

Sophia nodded. "I suppose."

"No, Mama." Annie leaned around into Sophia's line of vision. "We'll make it. We'll be fine."

"You were always the strongest." Sophia touched Annie's cheek. "Your father would have been proud of the way you've turned out."

Annie sat back, wondering how proud he would have been if he'd seen her in the cookhouse with Josh. Just what Sophia needed—*two* unwed, pregnant daughters.

"Let's take that walk-through," Sophia suggested, rising from the rocker, "before your Mr. Douglas arrives."

While Sophia put Hannah in her crib, Annie checked on the older children. She'd had them take baths this morning and dress properly in anticipation of Mr. Douglas's visit. Annie herself had even put on her green dress for the occasion and swept her hair up atop her head.

The children looked up from the puzzles scattered among them on the floor.

"Can we go out and play?" Drew asked.

"Not yet. I don't want you to get dirty before you've met your father's guest."

The three children grumbled.

"How about if I read you a story?" Annie suggested. "We could play a game together and pass the time more quickly."

"No," Ginny told her. "We want to work puzzles."

"I'm tired of working these dang ol' puzzles,"
Drew said, tossing several pieces into the air.

"Me, too," Cassie said. "Can't we play a game,
Ginny? Please."

"No!" Ginny glared up at Annie. "We don't
want to play anything with you."

Annie's heart softened at the sight of Ginny's angry face. She bent down and touched the child's
shoulder. Ginny jerked away, but Annie placed a
little kiss on her forehead just the same.

"If you change your mind, honey, let me know,"
Annie said, then left the room.

Sophia and Annie checked on the room set aside
for Mr. Douglas at the end of the hallway. Sparkling
windows, fresh linens, sachets in the drawers, not a
speck of dirt or dust to be seen—Sophia pronounced
it ready for company, and they moved on.

Downstairs, as they walked through each room,
Sophia ran her finger along the tables and around
the lamp chimneys, looking for dirt. She found nothing. "This is a lovely home," she said finally, standing in the parlor.

"Josh's wife decorated it."

"Lovely," Sophia said, "but hardly a home designed for children. All these expensive things don't
mix well with little ones."

"That's why they're not allowed downstairs,"
Annie said. "If this were my house, I'd—"

"Your house?"

Annie blushed. "I meant…"

Sophia looked harder at her. "Annie, is something else going on here?"

"No, of course not."

"Something between you and—"

"Georgia!" Annie caught a glimpse of the maid hurrying past the parlor door. "Is something wrong?"

"I just saw a wagon coming up the road. It's that Mr. Douglas fella, I'll bet," Georgia said. "Should I go fetch Mr. Ingalls?"

"No," Annie said, trying not to glance at her mother's suspicious expression. "I'll find him. You greet our guest."

"Me?" Georgia's eyebrows bobbed upward. "I don't know nothing about greeting a guest. What am I supposed to say to him?"

Annie turned to her mother. "Would you do it? Please? Josh said he'd stay close to the house today, since Mr. Douglas is expected. I'll find him and be back in just a few minutes."

"Of course," Sophia said, patting the back of her upswept hair. "Come along, Georgia."

Annie went the other way, toward the rear of the house. She stopped by the cookhouse and told Mrs. Royce their guest had arrived, and asked her to prepare refreshments, then took the back steps outside.

The afternoon was warm. Annie shaded her hand against the sun burning brightly in the blue sky.

Where was Josh?

"Must be nice…"

Josh leaned against the stall gate, rubbing his

horse's neck. The stallion muzzled him, snorting and blowing hot breath against his shirt.

"Pretty simple life you lead, boy," Josh murmured. "When you're in need of a little female companionship, you don't care who's around, who might be watching. You don't even care which mare it is."

The horse wasn't particular. Josh was.

Not that he could do anything about it.

These last few nights he might have enjoyed dreaming about Annie and what had nearly happened between them in the cookhouse; dreaming about it was as close as he figured he would—or should—get.

Instead, he'd dreamed about Night Hawk and the eagle again. Eagle feathers everywhere. Not one image of Annie, naked, feathered or otherwise.

"Hell, maybe I should ride out and see Night Hawk," Josh said to his horse. "What do you think, boy?"

Josh had a lot of respect for Night Hawk and the ways of his people. They seemed to know things, understand things that escaped others. Surely his friend could help him interpret his dream. Maybe then he'd stop having it. Maybe he'd feel settled.

Even without Annie in his dreams he'd awakened tight and achy. He'd spend most of his days lately that way, too.

There was nothing Night Hawk could do about that.

Only one person could alleviate that problem.

But to turn to her meant—what?

Josh sighed heavily in the silent barn. He didn't know what it meant. He couldn't get much further than thinking about how much he wanted her. How much he looked forward to seeing her, talking with her. How at night he wished she'd come down to his study like she used to, sit across from his desk and discuss her day and his.

She'd do it if he asked. But Josh wouldn't—couldn't—ask.

Something held him back. Something. He didn't know what.

Anger grew inside Josh as he stepped away from the stall. But just who he was mad at, he didn't know. With Annie? Lydia? Himself?

All he knew was that things had been going along as planned. His life had been heading down the track he'd picked out. Now everything was different. Now he was questioning things that he'd settled in his mind years ago. Now everything had been turned upside down.

Including him.

"Josh?"

Annie stepped into the barn through the open doorway. Josh's heartbeat stumbled at the sight of her.

At that instant, he didn't care if he and everything else around him was turned upside down or not.

How pretty she looked. Somehow, Annie made that plain, simple dress she had on look special. Her hair was tucked up with little wisps curling around her face.

He'd avoided her since the night in the cookhouse. Now, seeing her all done up in her female trappings, layered in petticoats, corsets and God knew what else, all he could think of was her standing in front of him wearing only his shirt. How he'd reached under it, pulled that towel off of her, then—

"Josh? Are you feeling all right? You look a little flushed."

Damn right he was flushed. Flushed, and then some.

"What's wrong? Are the children all right?" he asked out of habit. Lydia had never sought him out unless something bad had happened.

"Mr. Douglas is here," Annie said, waving toward the house. "My mother stopped by to visit, so I left her to greet him. I hope that's all right?"

"Why wouldn't it be?"

"Because…" Annie's words trailed off as if she had something else to say but didn't want to.

She was keeping things from him. Josh could see it so easily. He'd been content to let that go, in the past, but now it annoyed him more and more.

"No, that's fine," Josh said. "Your mama's welcome here anytime."

"Everything's prepared," Annie said, as they walked toward the house together. "Mrs. Royce is making refreshments."

"I don't mind telling you," Josh grumbled, "that when this visitor is gone, it will suit me fine."

"Not planning to invite anyone else here?" Annie asked. "No more craftsmen, inventors or relatives?"

Josh shrugged. "I've got kin in Germany I hear from every so often. The Gunther Ingalls branch of the family might come out this way, but not anytime soon, I don't think."

As they approached the back door, Georgia yanked it open, wringing her hands.

"Lordy, Annie, you'd better git in the parlor right now," she exclaimed.

Josh pushed past the two women. Annie hurried after him.

In the parlor, she found her mother prone on the settee. A tall, white-haired man in a respectable suit—obviously Thomas Douglas—stood over her, fanning her with his hat.

"She's fainted," he said. "Sophie's fainted."

Chapter Twenty-One

"How's your mother?" Josh asked, as Annie walked into his study.

When Sophia had roused from her faint, Josh had helped take her upstairs to Annie's room.

"She's resting."

Josh rose from behind his desk and guided Annie to the leather settee in the corner. She looked tired, worried. When they sat down together, he wanted to take her in his arms, rest her head on his shoulder. For a moment, Annie looked as if she wanted the same. But instead, she sat at the far end, keeping her distance from him.

"Mr. Douglas is in his room, too," Annie said. "Did he say anything to you?"

"Nothing," Josh said. "Did your mother tell you why she fainted?"

"She only said that she and Mr. Douglas knew each other years ago in Missouri."

"And that caused her to faint?" Josh asked.

Annie pressed her lips together. "Apparently."

"Doesn't that strike you as odd?" Josh asked. "Aren't you curious to know more?"

"Of course," Annie said. "But Mama is being very closemouthed about it."

Josh nodded slowly. "Makes you realize, doesn't it, how little you can know about another person."

"No, not really," Annie said, and sprang off the settee. "Could I borrow a wagon to take Mama home? I don't think she's up to the walk."

Josh studied her for a moment, sure she'd changed the subject on purpose. Whenever he mentioned her past or her family, Annie clammed up.

"Isn't she staying for supper?" Josh asked.

"No."

"I'd think she and Douglas would like to visit awhile. Catch up."

Annie shook her head. "I don't think this is a good time for that. She's not feeling well."

Josh rose from the settee. "I've decided to ask your mother to act as hostess for the party. I'm sure she'll be good at it and I don't really want to ask Mrs. Baird. Do you think Sophia will feel up to it?"

"No," Annie said quickly. "She can't do that."

"She'll be better by then, don't you think?"

"It's not that."

"Then what is it?" Josh frowned, a little annoyed by her evasiveness. "Annie, why is it I always get the feeling there are things you're not telling me?"

Annie looked up sharply, her cheeks coloring.

"Mama can't act as your hostess because she's not invited to the party."

"Not in—"

"Not invited," Annie told him. "Mrs. Flanders didn't include her on the guest list."

"That's crazy," Josh said, waving his hands. "I told Camille—"

"A verbal invitation to a child does not constitute an invitation."

Josh's brows drew together. "For a simple farm girl, you know a hell of a lot about etiquette."

"You don't have to be a New York socialite to know an invitation is needed to attend a party," she told him.

"I suppose not," Josh admitted. "But, look, I want your family to be there, especially if your mama already knows Douglas. Tell them to come."

Annie didn't look nearly as pleased by the invitation as he expected she would. If anything, it appeared to cause her more discomfort.

"I'll tell Mama," Annie said, "but I don't know if she'll come."

When she started to move away, Josh caught her arm. He turned her chin to face him and saw tears standing in her eyes.

"Annie—"

"I have to see about the children."

She tried to pull away, but Josh held her in place, resisting the urge to take her in his arms.

"Annie, is there something you want to tell me, something you want to talk about?" he asked softly.

Those big blue eyes of hers gazed up at him for a few seconds, vulnerability evident in their depths. Her lips trembled. Josh knew—knew! She wanted to tell him whatever it was that troubled her. He could feel it.

But then Annie blinked back her tears and pressed her lips together, drawing on some invisible well of strength.

"I have to take care of the children," she murmured.

Josh stood by the settee and watched her walk from the room, her shoulders square, her head high. He felt as if he'd failed somehow. As if he'd had her within his grasp and she'd slipped away.

"Damn …"

"Good day, Mrs. Baird," Josh said, striding into his parlor.

"Good day, Mr. Ingalls." Seated on the settee, Eleanor stretched out her hand, allowing him to touch her gloved fingers. "I'm glad I caught you at home…this time."

Josh sat down in the chair across from her, wondering if the woman somehow knew that the last time she'd come to call he'd hidden out in the barn—with Annie.

"I've been busy since Mr. Douglas arrived. We were just working in the study," Josh explained, hoping the hint would hurry her along.

"Then let me come right to the point," Eleanor said, leaning forward slightly.

Josh almost said, 'Good!' but managed to hold his tongue. He didn't have much patience for Eleanor Baird, or the daughter she had been trying for the last six months to push off on him.

Yet despite her promise to be brief, Eleanor leaned back on the settee, making herself comfortable. Josh held in a groan.

"About your Mr. Douglas and this party you've planned for him tomorrow evening," Eleanor said. "I woke this morning knowing—knowing, I tell you—knowing in my heart that I must come here today."

When she didn't continue, Josh was obligated to ask, "And why is that?"

"Mrs. Flanders has left you," Eleanor said, as if the woman had died, "and I can only imagine the difficulties you've had arranging for this party."

Josh shrugged. "Actually, things are going fine."

Eleanor pursed her lips, as if she pitied him not having enough sense to know things weren't going well. "Anyway, I woke this morning knowing I had to come over here and check on the preparations. I owe it to your dear wife, God rest her soul."

"Lydia?"

"She was a well-bred, gracious lady, whom I counted as a dear friend," Eleanor said. "I simply couldn't live with myself if I didn't make sure her home was ready to receive guests."

"I—"

"And to step in as hostess for the party." Eleanor

tilted her head. "You don't have a hostess, do you?"

"I'd asked Mrs. Martin to—"

"Sophia Martin?"

"Yes, but she couldn't do it."

Eleanor harrumphed. "I should think not. Not given her family's...circumstances."

"Circumstances?"

"That daughter of hers," Eleanor said, pursing her lips as if she'd tasted something sour.

"Annie?"

"No, no, not that one."

"Camille?"

"No, the other one." Eleanor waved her hands, dismissing the subject, and pushed herself up from the settee. "So, since I'm here, I'd like to speak with your cook, just to make certain everything is properly planned for tomorrow night's festivities. If I may?"

Josh followed Eleanor as she headed toward the cookhouse, her head swiveling back and forth as she assessed every room, every piece of furniture they passed. By the time they got to the cookhouse, Josh wasn't sure who he was more annoyed with, Eleanor or Annie.

Annie had another sister? She'd never mentioned her, had she? Why? And what were these "circumstances" surrounding her—and Annie's family?

In the cookhouse, Mrs. Royce stood at one of the worktables, Annie beside her, the recipe book between them. It didn't surprise Josh to see Annie there. He'd caught glimpses of her conferring with the cooks and the other servants for days now.

"Good day, Mrs. Baird," Annie said, glancing back and forth between their visitor and Josh.

"I'll be acting as hostess for the party tomorrow night," Eleanor announced, "together with Constance."

"Your daughter?" Annie asked.

"Of course." Eleanor butted between Annie and Mrs. Royce. "Now, let's see what we have here."

Annie was forced to move aside, but under no obligation to stay in the cookhouse and watch the woman she didn't particularly like take over the party she'd spent days planning and preparing for.

Josh blocked her path as she headed for the stairs. "Annie, wait—"

She darted around him and hurried upstairs, refusing to answer him.

She was halfway up the first staircase when Josh called her name again. She turned back and saw him standing at the foot of the stairs.

"Annie, I want—"

"Leave me alone," Annie insisted.

"No."

"Go," she told him, "before Eleanor Baird sees you and gets any ideas."

He frowned. "I don't give a damn what Eleanor Baird thinks."

"Well, I do." Annie hurried up the stairs.

He didn't follow her. She should have been glad, since that's what she wanted, what had to happen.

Still, a sense of loss crept through Annie as she walked out on the back balcony.

Leaning on the railing, looking out over the farm, Annie realized how comforting this spot in the Ingalls house had become. The fields, the crops, the livestock, the outbuildings and equipment—all the things Josh had built from the raw land. She felt some of the pride he surely had in his accomplishments. He'd achieved great things.

So, in view of all that, wasn't it only natural that Eleanor Baird and her daughter would act as hostesses for his party?

Annie slumped into one of the rockers and leaned her head back. Next to the Ingalls family, the Bairds were the most prominent in the settlement. Both families had lived here and known each other for years. They were the same type of people.

And there was no scandal swirling around the Baird family.

When Annie had told her mother that Josh had asked her to act as hostess for his party, Sophia had been pleased. For a flash of a second, Annie had seen the excitement in her mother's eyes, the glint that hadn't been there in years.

Then, just as quickly, it was gone. Annie knew why, just as her mother knew.

Sophia couldn't possibly act as hostess, not considering the way everyone in the settlement felt about the Martin family. It would only cause more talk. Sophia would be overstepping her place, flaunting herself to the neighbors. Talk would spread even more. Their cousin Angus might go so far as to banish them from his home. If that happened, Annie didn't know where they'd move next. Or what it might do to her mother. Or how Annie would pay for Camille's school if she lost her job.

Annie drew her legs up and rested her palms on the knees of her trousers. She probably should have worn a dress today, but didn't. She pressed her lips together, thinking she might cry. She seldom cried. But lately, her heart had ached each time she saw Josh, or heard him speak, or heard anyone else mention his name. Even walking through the house—his house—made her heart hurt.

She loved him. She loved him, his children, his home. And obviously—quite obviously—her love wasn't wanted or needed.

Eleanor was taking over the party. The children couldn't make it any more plain that they wanted nothing to do with her.

And Josh…Annie's heart ached anew thinking of him. She didn't know where she stood with him. She certainly didn't know how she'd ever get through the party tomorrow evening, forced to watch Constance Baird standing at his side.

Annie pushed herself out of the rocker and swiped at her nose, forcing back the urge to cry, not sure how she'd get through tomorrow night, how she'd survive the scandal her sister had caused, how she'd help her mother or send Camille away to school if she lost her job.

At the moment, all the problems riding on her

shoulders overwhelmed her. She could barely stand up under the crush of them.

Leaving the balcony, Annie realized that she hadn't heard from the children in a while. She'd left them in their room earlier, with Georgia watching Hannah in the nursery, while she went downstairs to talk with Mrs. Royce. She hadn't meant to stay away so long. Leaving the children to their own devices was usually not a good idea.

Glancing down the hallway, she was relieved to see them still in their room, playing quietly together on one of the beds.

Annie went into her own room. A little mewl slipped through her lips as she saw her wardrobe cupboard standing open.

And on the floor in front of it lay a heap of shredded fabric that had been her three dresses.

Chapter Twenty-Two

A sob tore from Annie's throat as she collapsed to the floor. Tears streamed down her face. She picked through the debris.

Strips of brown, chucks of blue, ribbons of green. Big pieces, small pieces. Ragged ones.

Her dresses. All three of them. The only dresses she owned in the world.

Annie lifted a fragment of blue. Her blue dress. Her favorite. The one made from the fabric her mother had scrimped and saved to buy for her.

Another anguished cry tore from Annie's throat. She didn't bother to wipe away her tears, just let them fall.

The children. The children had done this. They'd found scissors and pulled the ultimate prank on her.

Annie sobbed harder. She'd tried to take proper care of them. But the children didn't like her, didn't want her around. She'd failed. Miserably.

She didn't belong in the Ingalls house. She should

never have taken the job. She was wrong, so wrong to have tried. She should have stayed away, minded her own business. Look where her nosiness had gotten her.

"Miss Annie?"

Through the blur of tears, she spotted the three children standing in the doorway to the nursery, looking guilty and scared.

"It was all Ginny's idea!" Cassie shouted, and raced to Annie. She threw herself into Annie's lap and burst into tears.

"Yeah, it was Ginny's idea," Drew said. His bottom lip poked out, then trembled. Finally, he hopped onto Annie's lap, too, and began to cry.

Annie sobbed with them, hugging them against her.

Ginny stomped over to them, furious. "It was supposed to be funny! You were supposed to laugh!"

Sniffling, Annie rocked Cassie and Drew gently.

"You aren't supposed to cry!" Ginny shouted. "You're supposed to leave!"

Annie held the two sobbing children and looked up at Ginny's angry face. "I don't want to leave, Ginny. I want to stay. Forever. I love you all."

Tears puddled in Ginny's eyes. She gulped and sniffed, holding them in.

Annie reached out her hand. Ginny stood there a second longer, then burst into tears and collapsed on Annie's lap.

Still sobbing herself, Annie held all three of the

children as tightly as she could. They clung to her, wiggling and squirming to get closer.

The door to her bedroom burst open and Josh strode into the room. He did a double take at the sight of them. "What the devil is going on in here?"

Annie and the three children kept crying. Next door in the nursery, Hannah started to wail.

He looked down at the four of them in horror. "Annie, what happened? What's wrong?"

"N-nothing's wrong."

"But..." Josh flapped his arms at his sides, then plowed his fingers through his hair. Finally, he stomped into the nursery and came back with the screaming baby tucked under one arm.

"Annie, for chrissake, will you tell me what's going on?"

When he got nothing but sobs in reply, Josh dropped to the floor in front of her, sitting cross-legged, their knees almost touching. Cassie launched herself at him, throwing her arms around his neck. Drew did the same. Annie pulled Hannah into her own arms as Ginny crawled onto her father's lap. Josh reeled back, stunned, unsure of what to do. Finally, he closed his arms around the three of them.

Annie cradled the baby against her shoulder, rocking and patting her back as she wiped away her own tears.

Josh looked at her over the heads of his sniffling children. "Have I mentioned lately what a great job you're doing with the children?"

Annie gulped, her tears turning into laughter.

A few minutes later, when the children settled down, Josh asked, "Does somebody want to tell me what's going on in here?"

"Miss Annie loves us!" Cassie announced.

Josh frowned, as if Cassie's explanation only complicated things for him. He nodded toward the pile of shredded fabric.

"What's this all about?" he asked.

The children looked at Annie with trepidation. She smiled. "I'm teaching them to sew."

Josh raised an eyebrow. "To sew?"

"Yes," she told him. "Right, children?"

"Right," Ginny said.

"Oh, yes, Papa," Cassie swore solemnly.

"I don't want to learn to do no dang sewing," Drew complained, dragging his shirtsleeve across his nose.

They all sat there on the floor, tears and sniffles finally drying up.

Cassie looked up at Josh. "We love you, too, Papa," she said, and kissed his cheek.

At first Josh looked uncomfortable, unsure of what to do. Then he grinned and kissed each child on the forehead.

"How about if we all go down to the cookhouse?" Annie suggested. "I happen to know there's lemonade and fresh baked cookies down there."

The children clambered to the feet and headed out the door. Neither Josh nor Annie moved. They just looked at each other, a grin lingering on Josh's lips.

"I don't remember ever holding all of them at once before," he said.

"They're wonderful children."

He nodded toward the heap of fabric beside them. "You're sure about that?"

"Hold your daughter," Annie said, passing Hannah to him. She got to her feet and poured water into the basin at the washstand in the corner.

Josh followed. "Annie, I don't like it when you don't tell me things."

"It's nothing for you to concern yourself with," she said, splashing water onto her face. "If it were important, I'd tell you."

He looked at her, seemingly judging her answer, trying to decide if he believed her. "I don't like being lied to."

"I understand," Annie said, drying her face on a towel. She pulled Hannah from his arms. "Will you come downstairs for lemonade and cookies with the children?"

He shrugged. "Sure."

A sense of contentment came over Annie as she walked down the stairs, the baby in her arms, Josh two steps behind her, knowing the children waited in the cookhouse. All seemed right with the world, for the first time in a very long time. And what a wonderful feeling that was.

Another not so pleasant feeling came to Annie.

Halfway down the stairs she realized that now she had nothing to wear to the party.

*   *   *

Annie spent most of the day upstairs with the children. They played games, worked puzzles and let her read them two stories. Though the children were more open with her, Ginny still seemed a little reserved. Finally, she stopped Annie's reading.

"Miss Annie, I'm truly sorry about what we did to your dresses," she said.

Annie nodded. "Thank you for saying that, Ginny. I know things have been difficult for you children these last few months. I understand."

"I still feel bad," she said, ducking her head.

Annie touched her chin, bringing her face around. "You're not going to do anything like that again, are you?"

Ginny shook her head. "No, ma'am. Never."

"Then it's all settled," Annie said, opening the book again.

"But now you got no dresses," Drew said.

"It's all right. Not going to the party won't be the end of the world," Annie said, and she meant it. She'd gladly trade dozens of dresses for this opportunity to at last be close to the children.

She started to read again, but Ginny interrupted her.

"I know where there're some dresses," she said. "Pretty dresses. Lots of them."

Annie smiled indulgently, wondering if this were some flight of fancy. "Really? Where?"

"Where, Ginny?" Cassie asked.

Ginny smiled secretively. "You know."

Cassie thought for a moment and looked at her brother. Then both their faces lit up.

"Let's show her," Drew said.

"Come on, Miss Annie," Cassie said. "Wait till you see!"

The three children pulled Annie to her feet and led her by the hand down the hallway to one of the bedrooms. Annie stopped outside the door.

"Wasn't this your mother's room?" she asked, remembering what Georgia had told her.

"The dresses are in here," Ginny said, reaching for the doorknob.

"No," Annie said. "I couldn't possibly wear your mother's dresses. It wouldn't be right."

"But they're not," Ginny insisted, and opened the door. "They're not Mama's dresses."

"Wait," Annie said. "Is it all right if you go in? I mean, are you allowed?"

"Sure," Cassie said.

"Papa don't care," Drew told her. "We can go in anytime we want. He said so."

An unnatural silence hung over the room when they walked inside. It smelled faintly musty from being closed up so long.

This was a lady's room. Immediately, Annie saw Lydia's hand at work here, in the graceful carved furniture, delicate wallpaper, floral coverlet, elegant figurines and paintings on the walls.

"Back here." Ginny opened a door on the other side of the room.

Annie expected to find a passageway connecting

to Josh's room, but saw another room instead. In it hung rows and rows of women's clothing. Hat boxes and dozens of pairs of shoes were stacked on shelves.

The children ran into the room, but Annie didn't. "These are your mother's things. I can't—"

"No," Ginny insisted. "Look here."

In the back of the room sat several large wooden crates. Ginny and Drew lifted off the top of one. Inside, beneath layers of thin paper, lay bundles of the most exquisite garments Annie had ever seen.

"Mama ordered them from the East, back before Hannah was born," Ginny explained. "She showed them to me when they arrived. They were supposed to be gifts for our cousins in Pennsylvania."

"She had them sent here?"

"Mama wanted to see them first, make sure they were all right," Ginny said. "There're lots of dresses in here. All sorts of pretty things. Want to see?"

Annie couldn't help herself. She sank to her knees alongside the children, carefully going through the crate. Her heart swelled. She'd never seen so many fine things in her life, not even when she was young, when her papa was alive and could provide for them. Silk, taffeta, satin. A cashmere shawl. Embroidered trimmings, flounces, ruffles and netting. Each and every item was absolutely gorgeous.

"Do you like them?" Ginny asked.

"They're wonderful," Annie said, feeling slightly breathless. "Your mother had exquisite taste."

"Then wear one," Ginny said.

"No." Annie sat back, hardly able to speak the word, her heart yearned so badly for the clothing. "I can't."

"Papa won't care," Ginny said.

She shook her head. "No. I really shouldn't."

"You could ask Papa," Cassie said.

Annie looked at the crates of clothing, then at the children's hopeful faces. What to do? She wanted to go to the party, especially since her mother and sister had agreed to go since Sophia and Mr. Douglas already knew each other, and she did need something other than her trousers to wear. If the clothing had belonged to Lydia, she wouldn't even have considered wearing it. But the garments were intended for distant cousins. And they were gorgeous. Positively gorgeous.

"Well," Annie said, biting her lower lip. "I guess it wouldn't hurt to ask."

"We'll come with you," Ginny said.

"No, I think I'd better talk with your father alone," Annie said. She knew Josh would speak frankly to her, but might not with the children present. "I'll be back in a bit."

Annie wasn't even sure she could find Josh to ask him about the clothes. He and Thomas Douglas had kept busy riding over the farm and discussing business.

Before she went downstairs, Annie checked on Hannah. Georgia had her out on the back balcony.

"Do you know where Mr. Ingalls is?" Annie asked.

"I seen him and that Mr. Douglas fella heading down to the barn a while ago," Georgia said, waving in that direction. "'Course, I've had my hands full with this little lady. I might have missed them riding out."

It was a place to start.

Annie walked down to the barn and went inside. Two workers were there cleaning stalls.

"Is Mr. Ingalls here?" she asked.

One of them nodded and pointed upward, toward the loft.

Since Annie didn't want to shout her request up to him, she climbed the ladder, stopping just as her head poked through the opening in the wooden floor.

Thin shafts of light beamed through the cracks between the wall boards. Exposed timbers criss-crossed the A-frame roof. Hay covered the floor.

She located Josh off to her left, moving the hay around with a pitchfork. His shirt was off. He'd tied the sleeves of his long johns around his waist and pulled his suspenders in place again. Sweat rolled down the hard muscles of his back. His arms flexed and bulged as he worked.

And Lydia had a separate bedroom?

Annie grabbed the ladder, stunned by her own thoughts. Gracious, such a reaction.

But Josh had held her in those strong arms of his. He'd pressed that hard chest against her. She'd touched those muscles of his in the cookhouse that night. How could she not have such a reaction?

Annie heard the voices of the two men below and came to her senses. Goodness, here she stood ogling her employer.

She didn't want the men to see her climb into the loft with Josh, and possibly start more talk about her, so she stayed where she was on the ladder.

"Josh?" she called.

He looked up from his work and turned to face her. Sweat sparkled in the glistening dark hair on his chest.

"What's wrong?" he asked.

"Nothing," she said. "I came to ask you something."

Josh propped the pitchfork against the wall and pulled off his gloves, not unduly disturbed by this disruption in his work. "Ask away."

She glanced around, realizing he was alone in the loft. "Where's Mr. Douglas?"

"He borrowed a horse and rode into the settlement to pick up some things."

"I see." Annie cleared her throat. "Anyway, what I wanted to ask you about is that, well, you see, I don't have anything to wear—"

Josh tensed. He rose slightly on his toes and craned his neck, trying to see more of her. "So, you're…naked?"

"Of course not," Annie told him. She climbed up a few more steps on the ladder until he could see her to the waist. Still, the way he looked at her, she might as well have been naked.

She hurried on. "Anyway, the children showed me some dresses packed away at the house. Clothes they say your wife commissioned for her cousins back East. They thought I might wear one of them for the party tomorrow night, but I wanted to ask you first."

Josh pulled off his hat, ran his forearm across his sweaty brow and settled his hat in place again. He looked at her for a long moment, then shook his head.

"No."

Chapter Twenty-Three

"No? Why not?" she demanded. Annie would never have had the nerve to question Josh's decision if he hadn't looked so arrogant standing there, looking down at her.

"Because I said so," he told her. "If there were any more to the story that I felt you needed to know, I would have told you."

"But—"

"What's wrong?" he asked, not bothering to keep the smirk from his face. "Don't you like being told what you should and should not have knowledge of?"

Annie paused, her rising anger simmering now. Wasn't this exactly what she'd done to him time and time again? Refused to give him details of things the children had done when he'd specifically asked for them?

"I know what you're doing," she told him. "You're just trying to get back at me."

Josh walked closer. "Yep. I'd say that was true."

"But what you're doing is *completely* different from what I was doing," Annie insisted.

"How do you figure that?"

"Well…" Annie fumed a moment. "It just is, that's all."

"Oh, okay. I guess that explains everything," Josh said. He dropped to the floor of the loft, letting his legs dangle through the opening near Annie.

"So does that mean I can wear one of the dresses?" Annie asked, giving him a quick, sweet smile.

"No," he told her. "Not until you tell me what the children did that had all five of you crying."

Annie huffed. "Josh, you're making way too much of this."

"I don't like secrets."

They glared at each other for a long, tense moment. Finally, Annie relented.

"All right. The children ruined my dresses," she said. "But I don't want you to punish them. Really, it was for the best. They were just testing me and, finally, I passed. We're getting along much better already. Ginny is the one who offered me the clothing."

Josh seemed reluctant to believe her, but gradually, his frown faded. "All right. I'll accept that."

"And the clothing?"

His frown returned. "Is there anything else you feel I should know?"

Josh gazed at her with such intensity Annie nearly

melted on the spot. How tempting to tell him everything, to be relieved of this burden she'd carried for so long. He'd understand, wouldn't he?

Maybe. Probably.

But what if he didn't?

"Nothing," Annie said softly, and shook her head. "There's nothing else I should tell you."

"All right, then," he said, getting to his feet. "Wear the clothes, if you want. Someone should get some use out of them."

"Thank you," she said.

"You're welcome."

She started back down the ladder.

"Annie?" Josh called.

She stopped and looked up at him leaning over the opening.

"You're sure?" he asked. "There's nothing else you want to tell me?"

"No," she stated, and hurried down the ladder.

How much could a man take?

Josh tossed the diagrams on his desk and turned in his chair. How was he supposed to concentrate on his work with all that noise going on outside? All that laughter? All that fun?

Through the window he saw the morning sunlight stream through the trees, casting shadows on the side yard. The children played there, with Annie.

He'd watched them for some time now, catching glimpses of them when he was supposed to be studying the diagrams of the combination harvester

Thomas Douglas had given him. It hadn't helped any that Douglas had left earlier this morning on another errand and hadn't returned.

Annie and the children had decided to put up a tent of sorts under the trees. He'd seen them come from the barn, loaded down with odds and ends. Under Annie's direction, they had strung a rope between two trees, pinned horse blankets to it, fanned them out and secured them with rocks, forming a tent.

Such patience Annie had. It had taken at least two tries—sometimes more—for the children to accomplish each facet of the tent raising. But she stood by calmly, showing them what to do, encouraging them, laughing along with them. They'd sung songs together. She'd chased after them, at times, until they squealed.

After a trip into the house, they were all settled inside the tent now, playing with the toys they'd brought outside. Josh couldn't see inside, just its sides bulging occasionally.

He could have gone outside himself and had the tent put up in a matter of minutes. It had taken some patience on his part not to do it.

But he liked watching them. All of them. Annie included.

He couldn't remember when he'd heard his children laugh so much. How long had it been? Months, surely. Josh couldn't say for certain they'd laughed that much even before their mother died.

Annie laughed along with them. Easily, she could

have been one of them. But he'd seen the watchful eye she kept on all the children.

Up until now, Josh had been content to hide out in his study this morning. With the party scheduled for tonight, the house staff was everywhere, cleaning things that already looked clean, arranging this or that. He didn't know what they were doing, really. Mrs. Royce had been up since before dawn cooking. Josh was afraid that if he poked his nose out of his study one of them would pounce on him, ask him a question about the menu or the flowers or something. But all he'd seen of the staff, except when working, was when one of them had occasionally gone into the side yard and talked with Annie about something. He didn't know what that was all about, either.

A burst of laughter floated in through the window—sweet children's laughter. Josh looked at the diagrams waiting on his desk, then out the window again. He pushed himself out of his chair and went outside.

The tent wasn't tall enough for even the children to stand up in, so Josh knelt at one end and looked inside. A quilt was spread over the grass. Annie was at the far end, holding Hannah on her lap. The children sat cross-legged amid a clutter of dolls, books and toys.

"Papa!" Cassie exclaimed, seeing him first.

He smiled, pleased that the children seemed glad to see him. "This is quite a tent you've made."

"It was Miss Annie's idea," Ginny said.

"Come inside, Papa," Cassie said. "We're having a tea party."

He saw then that each of the children held a doll and the cup and saucer from a miniature tea set. All the children, including Drew.

"Miss Martin, could I speak with you for a moment?" he asked.

Annie scooted out the opposite end of the tent, still holding Hannah in her arms. "Yes?"

Josh pressed his lips together thoughtfully and leaned close to her. "Why is my son holding a doll?"

"Because we're playing house."

"I see." Josh nodded, then said, "And why is my son playing house?"

"Because the rest of us are girls and that's what we wanted to play. He was outvoted."

"I see." Josh walked back to the tent entrance. "Drew! Come out here!"

The boy came out of the tent, looking warily up at his father. "I didn't do nothing wrong."

Josh caught Drew's shoulder and pulled him closer. "You're coming with me to the barn. I've got some chores I need your help with."

"Yeah?" Drew's face lit up. "You mean it?"

"Yes." Josh looked at Annie. "And after that we'll have us a chaw of tobacco and knock back a couple of whiskeys. Maybe ride into the settlement and find us some women."

Annie giggled, because she knew he was kidding.

"Fine, then. We ladies will continue with our tea party."

Josh had started to walk away with Drew when Annie called him back. The playfulness was gone from her face.

"You'll keep an eye on him, won't you?" she asked.

"I will," he said. Her concern over his son touched him in an unexpected way. "Oh, by the way. I found out the story behind your mother and Thomas Douglas."

At noon, Annie took the girls inside to eat. Mrs. Royce and her helpers crisscrossed the cookhouse in what could have been a well-choreographed ballet. Staying out of their way as best she could, Annie secured a plate of cold meat, vegetables, bread just out of the oven and a pitcher of milk. Just as she got everything situated, Josh and Drew came in. All the children looked surprised when Josh sat down with them.

"How did the chores go?" Annie asked, holding Hannah and her bottle in one arm and dishing out food for the children.

"Me and Papa did lots of work, huh, Papa?" Drew said, his face bright and earnest.

"We sure did," Josh said. Without asking, he took Hannah from Annie, freeing her to tend to the other children.

"Can I do chores with you, too, Papa?" Cassie asked.

"I can use all the help I can get," Josh told her. Cassie beamed with delight.

While they ate, the children chattered, the girls telling Josh about what they'd played in the tent, and Drew filling Annie in on the chores he'd done at the barn. Josh held Hannah as long as he could, but being unaccustomed to wrangling with a baby while trying to eat, he finally gave up and passed her back to Annie.

"Can we go outside and play some more?" Ginny asked, when they'd finished their meal.

"For a while," Annie said. "You'll all need baths and time to dress before guests arrive this evening."

When the children left the cookhouse, Annie turned to Josh. "Was it all right for Drew to go with them? Or were you planning to send him out to bring down a deer for supper?"

Josh chuckled. "I can see I do need to spend more time with him. And the girls, too."

"They'd like that," Annie said.

"This is nice," Josh said, waving his hand across the table. "Eating with the children."

"They didn't eat with you...before?"

"Occasionally," Josh said. "Did you get your dress for tonight taken care of?"

Annie couldn't help smiling. Camille had come by yesterday afternoon and, with the children, they'd gone through the crates of dresses and found two that needed minimal alterations.

"It's all taken care of," Annie said. "I found a dress for Camille, too. I didn't think you'd mind."

"It's fine," Josh said. He glanced down and saw that Hannah had fallen asleep in Annie's arms. "Do you want to take her upstairs?"

She shook her head. "Not until you tell me this story about my mother and Mr. Douglas. I've been dying to hear the details all morning."

"According to what Thomas told me, he and your mother knew each other when they were young. He courted her for a while."

Annie gasped. "He did? Really? He told you that?"

Josh nodded. "Seems they were serious about each other. He was about to ask for her hand when she broke off with him."

"But why?"

"He didn't know," Josh said.

"Or maybe he didn't want to say why?"

"No, I really think he was surprised, and hurt, by your mother's decision."

"Gracious…" Annie said, shaking her head. "I had no idea. No wonder she fainted when she saw him. A man she used to love, showing up out of the blue, so far from her home. Who'd have thought it?"

"I don't think Thomas is so willing to let bygones be bygones," Josh said.

"What do you mean?"

"Since he got here, he's spent a great deal of his time supposedly taking in the countryside and going into the settlement," Josh said.

"Do you think he's been going to see Mama instead?"

"Maybe," Josh said, lifting his shoulders. "Did Camille say anything about him coming over?"

"No. But we were so busy with the dresses she might not have thought about it."

Josh grinned. "Well, it should make for an interesting party tonight."

"Yes, it should." Annie rose from the table. "I'd better put Hannah to bed."

As she climbed the steps, she couldn't help but think how right Josh had been. The Martin women—the black-sheep family of the settlement—showing up at the party. The guest of honor smitten, possibly, with one of them. Another of them ensconced in the Ingalls household. Eleanor and Constance Baird acting as hostesses. Everyone who was anyone in the settlement looking on.

"Oh, yes," Annie murmured, "it should be quite a party."

Chapter Twenty-Four

"Annie?" Josh stuck his head out of his bedroom and looked up and down the hallway. "Annie! Are you up here?"

"Here," he heard her call. "In the children's room."

Grumbling, he moved to the doorway. Annie was inside helping the children dress. She had on her wrapper; her hair was down, caught with a loose ribbon at her nape. Some of Josh's foul mood left.

She looked over her shoulder as she knelt in front of Cassie. "What is it?"

"Can you do anything with this damn thing?" he asked, tugging on his cravat.

What remained of his ill temper evaporated as Annie stood in front of him, tying his cravat. He stretched his chin up but kept his eyes focused on her. She was so pretty to look at. Occasionally, her fingers brushed his throat. How soft she was. And her scent...Annie smelled delightful. Having her this close more than made up for having to dress in these uncomfortable clothes tonight.

Too soon, she stepped back and gave him a nod. "There. Perfect."

"If you say so." Josh tugged on it once more, then ran his finger around his starched collar.

"How's Mr. Douglas?" Annie asked, nodding toward his room down the hall. "I haven't seen him in a while. Does he need anything?"

"He's gone," Josh said. He leaned closer—because he wanted to, rather than had to. "Gone to get your mother. He borrowed the surrey."

"Really?" Annie's eyes widened. "I'm going to have to speak to Mama tonight and get to the bottom of this whole thing."

Josh slipped into the coat he'd brought with him, tugged at his vest and stood up straight, offering himself for inspection. "Do I look acceptable?"

"Oh, Papa, you look beautiful," Cassie declared.

He grinned down at her and ruffled her hair. "Thank you."

Annie took a moment or two longer to make her decision. She gazed at him critically, assessing his shoes, his trousers, his coat, his hair. Finally she smiled at him and offered a nod of approval.

"Beautiful. Just like Cassie said," she told him. "You'd better get downstairs. Guests will start arriving soon."

But Josh didn't want to go. He'd never been crazy about parties, though Lydia had given them often, but tonight it was more than that. Tonight, he didn't want to leave his children. Or Annie.

Despite all the years since his first child was born, Josh had spent little time with them, especially in their room. There was something almost magical here in this place, this room where his future grew. It seemed to tug at him, demand that he stay.

Or maybe it was Annie he felt. Josh watched as she slicked back Drew's hair, helped Cassie with her shoes, listening to Ginny at the same time. He'd felt so distant from his children, his home, until Annie came along. She seemed to hold them all together.

Josh frowned and took a step back, unexpectedly uncomfortable. "I'm going downstairs now," he said.

He wasn't sure Annie had heard him until she turned around and smiled.

"Yes, you should do that. I'll bring the children down in a little while," she said. "Georgia will stay in the nursery with Hannah."

Still Josh didn't move. Part of him wanted to stay—yearned to stay. Something else urged him to leave.

"Run along," Annie said, shooing him toward the door. "Your guests, remember?"

When he got downstairs, Josh hardly recognized his own house. Rooms were lit with extra lanterns and candles. Furniture had been shifted and musicians were tuning up in the parlor. The dining room table was laid out with platters and trays of food.

Josh didn't remember picking out so many of the

things Mrs. Royce and her staff had prepared. Some of the items he was sure he hadn't seen before.

He sampled one of the delicacies. It didn't taste familiar. "Is this one of the recipes I picked out?"

Mrs. Royce was at the opposite end of the table, dressed in a black uniform with a white, starched apron, arranging china plates and cutlery.

"No, sir. It's one of Miss Annie's," she murmured, concentrating on her task. "Goodness knows how we'd have gotten this occasion handled if it hadn't been for her taking charge."

Mrs. Royce hurried out of the room, leaving Josh to stare after her. Annie had helped with the party? She'd claimed she didn't know anything about it, but obviously she did. Why hadn't she told him?

Josh had no time to think about that because Eleanor and Constance Baird arrived. Eleanor, wearing a deep purple gown, and Constance, in emerald green, took over the house, dragging Josh with them as they assessed the party preparations.

"Excellent," Eleanor declared after she'd moved a few things around on the dining room table. "You two young people stay here while I check with the cook."

Eleanor disappeared, leaving Josh alone with Constance. She'd just started to bat her lashes at him when, thankfully, the first guest arrived.

A procession of neighbors and friends came through the front door as Josh stood sandwiched between the two Baird women, greeting them. Most of the folks he'd seldom seen in the past few months, up until Annie had insisted the family start going to church again. Now, having them in his home was a welcome feeling.

Thomas Douglas finally arrived with Sophia and Camille on his arms. Eleanor gushed over Thomas, welcoming him to the settlement, to the party, insisting he set aside some time to speak with her later. He seemed a little uncomfortable with his sudden celebrity.

When all the guests had finally arrived, Josh milled around the parlor talking with everyone. The men, most of them farmers, were very interested in hearing Josh's assessment of the combination harvester. He did his best to answer the questions, but his attention kept drifting to the staircase.

Where was Annie? Why hadn't she come down yet? Was there a problem with the children?

Since the Ingallses were hosting the party, it was acceptable for the children to come down for a while. They wouldn't stay long. Still, he was anxious to see them.

It didn't escape Josh's notice how attentive Thomas Douglas was to Annie's mother. He'd been surrounded by folks for quite a while now, sharing news from outside the settlement, but had kept Sophia by his side the whole time. She seemed content there, Josh decided.

Finally, the children came into the room. They looked scrubbed clean, crisp, starched and well dressed. A wave of pride wafted through Josh at seeing them.

Annie stepped into the parlor behind them, and his heart rose in his throat.

Her dress was sky-blue, highlighting the depths of her eyes. The full skirt had a double row of flounces at the hem, a single row at her sleeves. The wide neck revealed the curve of her shoulders. Her golden hair was caught up in back with rows of dangling sausage curls.

She looked beautiful.

Josh made his way through the crowd to her and couldn't resist dipping his gaze to take in her bare shoulders and the swell of her bosom.

"You look lovely," he said, knowing the words were inadequate, but unable to think clearly enough at the moment to come up with anything else.

"Thank you," she said, tilting her head. "It's by far the most beautiful thing I've ever worn."

"I don't think so." Josh shook his head. "I've seen you in something I like better."

"Surely you don't mean those trousers?"

Josh leaned closer and whispered, "The towel."

Her cheeks pinkened and she dipped her lashes. "Behave yourself, before you make me the talk of the party. Come along, children, it's time to meet our guests."

Josh trailed along behind her as she guided the children through the room, having them acknowledge most of the people. Cassie and Ginny were wide-eyed and excited; Drew, like most of the other males in the room, looked as if he'd rather be somewhere else.

But Annie was patient and gracious as she took the children around, holding Cassie's hand, urging Drew forward when necessary.

Two men drew Josh into a conversation as the musicians began to play. Several couples moved to the center of the parlor and began to dance. Josh glanced around, looking for Annie.

Where the devil was she? He wanted to dance with her. If she'd dance with him, he could get closer to her. He could touch her, have her all to himself.

The party wore on. Josh talked to his guests and wondered where Annie was. He finally spotted her again coming down the stairs.

"Is everything all right?" he asked, after he'd made his way to her.

"Just getting the children into bed," Annie explained. "They're a little keyed up, but I finally got them settled in."

"I know how that feels," Josh murmured. "Would you like to dance?"

For an instant, he knew she'd say yes. Annie's face brightened, causing his fingers to tingle. He itched to hold her in his arms.

Then she shook her head. "No, thank you. But you should dance with some of your other guests."

But he didn't want to dance with the other guests. He wanted to dance with Annie.

"That's all right," he said. "I didn't really want to dance, anyway."

"Oh."

"Could I get you some punch?" Josh asked. "I'm sort of thirsty myself."

"No, thank you. Help yourself, though."

"I'm not really all that thirsty."

"I see."

"I don't suppose you'd want anything to eat?" he asked.

"Not really."

"Me, either."

Josh rocked back and forth on his toes, looking out over his guests. Here Annie stood, right beside him, looking so damn touchable in that dress, and he couldn't do one thing about it. He couldn't remember when he had tried so hard to be nice to somebody—especially a woman. And he sure as hell didn't understand why she wouldn't let him.

"Excuse me," Annie said.

"But…"

She moved away before he could stop her, left him standing there admiring the sway of her skirt, the curve of her shoulders, her tight waist, teetering on the edge of embarrassing himself in front of his houseful of guests.

Josh strode into the dining room, took a look at the punch bowl in the center of the table, then went into his study and poured himself a brandy. He wasn't much of a drinker, but tonight, right now, it sounded good.

A timid knock sounded at the door. He glanced up, hoping it was Annie. Instead it was her mother. Josh set the glass aside.

"Can I speak with you a moment?" Sophia asked, coming into the room.

Sophia was still a nice-looking woman, tall and trim, with light hair that showed a few strands of gray. Annie favored her.

"Are you enjoying the party?" Josh asked.

"Yes, it's wonderful," Sophia said, without much enthusiasm. She took a breath. "I know you didn't plan it this way, but I wanted to thank you for bringing Thomas out here and into my life again. I know he told you about...about the two of us. Our... past."

"He seems very pleased to have found you again after all these years."

Sophia smiled faintly. "I was in love with Thomas all those years ago. He loved me, too. But I knew I couldn't marry him."

"Why not?"

"Money," Sophia said. "He was virtually penniless. I feared for what sort of future I'd have with him, what sort of life he could provide for our children. Reality won out. I married Annie's father instead."

"And now you regret that decision?"

Sophia shook her head. "It's funny what we give up. Often it's the thing we needed the most. Other times it's exactly the right thing to do. The trick, of course, is making the right decision. Either way, something is lost.

"Well, I'd better get back to the party," Sophia said, and left the study.

Her words seemed to echo in the room long after she'd gone. Josh sipped his brandy. What to hold on to and what to turn loose? That was the most difficult question.

Unbidden, the question slipped into his mind: had he made the right decisions in the past?

Josh tossed back the brandy and shook away the thought. He didn't want to think about that now. Maybe never.

Reluctantly, he went back to the party. Annie was still there, sitting with Camille, listening to the musicians. Friends came up and talked with him, but Josh could hardly keep his eyes off of Annie. Once or twice she looked at him, but glanced away just as quickly.

Finally, the evening wound down and guests departed. As Angus Martin left, he spoke quietly with Josh.

"I apologize for what's happened here," Angus said. "If I'd known Annie was intending to get a job with you, I'd have put a stop to it right away. I'm stuck with these woman and there's nothing I can do about it. But I wouldn't have allowed them to disgrace your home."

Angus moved away, leaving Josh dumbfounded. What the devil was he talking about?

Josh mumbled goodbyes to his other guests, thinking back over the evening. True, Annie and that dress of hers had been uppermost in his mind. But now, remembering what else had gone on, he realized something had been amiss.

Though Sophia had been at the guest of honor's side, few of the women had spoken to her. Camille had spent most of her time with Annie, not the other guests. Few of them had had much to say to Annie, even when she'd brought the children around.

What the devil was going on under his own roof that he didn't know about?

When the last guest thankfully departed, Josh took the stairs two at a time up to the children's room. He'd seen Annie go up earlier, and as he expected, found her in their room. She'd changed out of her dress already. Now she wore her wrapper, and her hair was loose on her shoulders. In the dim light of the wall lanterns, she checked each of the sleeping children, pulled up their covers, tucked in their feet.

"Annie?"

Her head came up quickly. She looked mildly surprised seeing him standing in the doorway, hearing the tone of his voice. She came closer.

"Come in here."

Josh took her hand, pulled her into his room, and closed the door.

Chapter Twenty-Five

"What's wrong?" Annie asked, standing just inside Josh's closed bedroom door. He didn't answer, but she heard his footsteps and saw his shadow moving through the room. A match sparked as he lit the lantern on the bureau.

She glanced back toward the door. "What's going on?"

"That's what I'd like you to tell me," Josh said.

He sounded upset, irritated. When he turned toward her, his face was grim.

"What are you talking about?" Annie asked, a little annoyed with him.

Josh pulled off his coat, then plucked open the buttons of his vest. "I told you from the beginning I don't like secrets."

"And?"

"And I don't think you've told me the truth about everything."

Annie folded her arms across her middle. "I don't know what you're talking about."

"What is it about your family?" he asked, slipping his cravat loose and tossing it aside. "Your uncle apologized tonight because you were working here. Why?"

"Perhaps you should ask him that."

"Damn it, Annie." Josh popped open the top button of his shirt and crossed the room to stand in front of her. "I didn't even know you had another sister. You claimed you couldn't help me with the party preparations, yet it seems you know all about such things."

"That's hardly a crime."

He leaned closer. "I trusted you to come into my home, to take care of my children, yet you can't tell me anything about yourself?"

"Why should I tell you more?" she demanded, her anger growing along with his. "I'm just the hired help around here. A servant."

Josh reeled back, stunned, and shook his head slowly. "No, Annie, you're not. You're much more than that."

"I know my place."

"I can assure you I've never kissed a servant," Josh told her. "I've not even kissed another woman in months, but I kissed you."

Annie turned her head away, her heart racing. How it had hurt to turn down his invitation to dance earlier this evening, when she desperately wanted to be in his arms. To see him with Constance Baird, when she ached to stand at his side. To be in his home, yet not a part of it.

Josh eased closer until the heat of his body reached hers. "I'd like to kiss you again," he whispered.

She forced her chin up, gazing at him. "You shouldn't."

"But I do."

Josh angled his head down and covered her mouth with his. Gently, he kissed her, winding his way inside her. He moaned softly and took her in his arms.

She braced her palms against his chest, wanting to push him away. She knew what he wanted. Knew, too, how she felt about him. How she loved him.

His familiar warmth spread over her, through her. His strong arms sapped her strength. Annie clung to him.

Suddenly it didn't matter what the settlement thought of her or her family. She loved Josh. She wanted this moment with him, regardless of the consequences. Annie looped her arms around his neck, rose on her toes and kissed him back.

He lowered his mouth, downward to the top button of her wrapper, then opened the fasteners and pushed it off her shoulders. It pooled on the floor around her feet. Josh kissed her again as he unbuttoned her night rail to her waist. He slid his hand inside and cupped her breast.

"Oh, Annie…" he moaned, easing the night rail off one shoulder and lowering his head.

Annie cradled his head against her, digging her

fingers into his hair. He kissed her mouth once more, hot and deep, then pulled his lips away.

"Annie…I want you."

She nodded. "I understand."

"You're sure?"

"Very," she whispered, and slid her palms across his shirt.

Josh groaned, swept her into his arms and carried her to his bed. He laid her down, yanked off his clothes, and stretched out beside her. Her night rail was open, her hair fanned across the pillow.

"You're beautiful," he whispered.

"Even without the towel?"

"Especially without the towel."

She came willingly into his arms, kissing him, touching him tentatively. How maddening it was to wait, to hold himself back. Annie didn't make it easy for him.

Josh slid his hand beneath the hem of her night rail, gliding his palm across her smooth flesh, then pulled it over her head. She came fully against him, touching him as he touched her, exploring, her hands and mouth wandering. Finally, when he could bear it no longer, he moved above her.

Annie's head spun as he kissed her face, her throat, her cheeks, and pressed himself into her. When she accepted him, he moved slowly, rocking gently against her. Warmth grew inside her, building steadily, until it suddenly gave way to waves of exquisite pleasure.

Josh wrapped his arms around her, struggling to

hold back until her head fell against the pillow. He moaned her name and pushed into her until he was spent.

Josh awoke with a start and shot straight up in bed. Beads of perspiration dampened his forehead. His heart hammered in his chest.

What time was it?

He glanced out the window. Only the faintest light showed, indicating dawn's approach.

Where was he?

Disoriented, he scanned the room.

A lantern burned on the bureau. Clothes were scattered across the floor.

Clothes?

His clothes. Annie's clothes. He remembered then.

Turning, he saw Annie sleeping soundly. He didn't recall how they'd gotten under the coverlet, yet it was pulled up now, barely covering the swell of her bare breasts.

Josh plowed his fingers through his hair, trying to slow his breathing.

That dream. That damn dream had awakened him.

It had come to him again, this time more vivid than before. Urgent and demanding.

But demanding what? What did it mean? He couldn't shake the feeling there was a message hidden in the dream. But what was it?

Sliding out of bed, Josh walked to the window.

Clouds gathered on the distant horizon. The air smelled sweet. It might rain today.

Annie mumbled in her sleep. He looked back at her but didn't see her beauty. Instead, a stab of regret sliced through him.

What the hell had he been thinking last night? Bringing Annie to his bed had seemed like the right thing to do—the only thing to do. But how could he have done such a thing when he still—

"Damn it..." Josh mumbled in the silent room.

He turned back to the window. He didn't know what to do, which way to turn. He needed help.

Now.

Annie came awake slowly to the scent of Josh on the bed linens. Curled on her side, facing the window, she lay still for a while in the silent room. Last night came back to her.

What had she done? She'd given herself to a man who'd promised her nothing, who hadn't even said he loved her.

She expected to feel regretful for her actions, but didn't. Instead, a warm glow filled her. The glow of the love she felt for one man. Josh.

Feeling a bit shy now, despite what they'd done last night, Annie tugged the coverlet closer and rolled over. She wanted to see Josh in the early morning light. She wanted to have that memory of him, regardless of what lay ahead.

But when she turned, Annie saw nothing but the cold, empty bed. Josh was gone.

* * *

She probably should have cried, Annie thought as she finished dressing in her room. To make love with a man, then find him gone in the morning was a hurtful thing. So why wasn't she crying?

Because she wasn't hurt. She was mad.

She'd sneaked out of Josh's room this morning and crossed the hall to her own room, praying no servants were up yet, that Thomas Douglas wasn't an early riser, that the children weren't awake. Thankfully, no one saw her.

By the time she'd bathed and dressed in her trousers, any hurt she felt—along with any tender feelings for Josh—had hardened to anger.

Annie checked on the children and was glad to see all four of them still sleeping. On her way downstairs, it occurred to her that perhaps there'd been an emergency of some sort. Some reason Josh had left in such a hurry.

But if he had, couldn't he have awakened her? Annie had no experience making love with a man, but it seemed to her the decent thing to do was for both partners to hang around until the morning.

Unless...

Annie paused on the bottom step. Unless he'd left because he was done with her.

Her heart sank to the pit of her stomach. What if that was the reason? What if last night had meant nothing to Josh?

"Miss Annie?"

Mrs. Royce crept down the hallway, looking tired

and weary. The staff was surely exhausted after last night's party. Today, they still needed to clean up, return the house to its former self. Much had to be done.

"There's a young woman waiting in the parlor," Mrs. Royce said.

"Here? Now? On a Sunday morning?"

Mrs. Royce shook her head as if she didn't understand it, either. "She's just arrived, looking for Mr. Ingalls. I can't find him anywhere. I think it's best that you talk to her."

An odd feeling crept up Annie's spine. "What does she want?"

Mrs. Royce didn't answer. She just turned and walked away.

Annie ventured into the parlor. The furniture was still in disarray from last night, chairs bunched together, the rug rolled back.

A young woman in traveling clothes sat on the edge of the settee. A satchel was at her feet. She looked weary and rumpled.

"Can I help you?" Annie asked.

She looked up, obviously relieved someone had arrived to talk to her, and got to her feet. "I'm Darla Talmadge. From the agency."

"Agency?"

"Yes," she said. "The employment agency in New York."

Annie stared at her, trying to make sense of what she'd said. "I don't understand."

Darla fished a dog-eared paper from her skirt

pocket and thrust it at Annie. "It's all right here. I'm expected."

"Expected?"

"Yes. I'm the new nanny."

Annie's breath left her in a huff. She shook her head. "No…"

"Yes." Darla pushed the paper toward her again. "I was sent for by Mr. Josh Ingalls."

Annie ran out of the room and out of the house.

Chapter Twenty-Six

The gray morning sky hung low and a mist rose from the lake as Josh pulled his horse to a stop. Just ahead on a small rise, ringed by woodlands, sat Night Hawk's log cabin. Smoke puffed from the stone chimney. Horses and foals grazed in the meadow. A young orchard grew nearby.

Peace and contentment drifted over Josh at the sight of his friend's home, leaving him faintly envious. Night Hawk had found the woman he loved. She loved him, too. They'd married.

Though their life together had gotten off to a rocky start—Marie was a white woman and the daughter of Colonel Lafayette at Fort Tye—their love had overcome those obstacles. They had a son now, Blue Hawk, and from what Josh had heard, Marie's father had given up his prejudices and become a proud and doting grandpa.

Josh urged his horse forward and dismounted, tying the reins to the railing in front of the cabin. The

door opened and Night Hawk strode onto the porch.
He wore trousers and a deerskin shirt; his long black
hair was pulled back and tied with a strip of leather.

The men shook hands, then embraced, pounding
each other's backs.

"How's Marie?" Josh asked, nodding toward the
cabin.

"Doing fine," Night Hawk said. "Sleeping right
now."

"And the baby?"

"Growing stronger every day," he said, pride evident in his voice.

The two men moved off the porch and walked
toward the lake. For a moment Josh questioned his
wisdom at coming here. He wasn't sure what he
wanted from Night Hawk. He wasn't even sure what
was wrong. Nothing was clear to Josh anymore.

Night Hawk stopped and touched his shoulder.
"You're troubled."

"Yes," Josh admitted. He pulled on the tight
muscles at the back of his neck. "It's this damn
dream I keep having."

Night Hawk smiled. "A dream? That's the worst
of your problems?"

"That," Josh said, "and a woman."

Night Hawk nodded wisely. "Tell me about this
woman."

"Annie Martin, the new nanny. She's…" Josh
wasn't sure what else to say. How could he explain
to his friend what Annie meant to him—to his family—when he didn't understand it fully himself?

"Annie is a special woman?" Night Hawk asked.

Josh nodded. "Very special." That much he was sure of.

"Tell me of your dream."

Annoyed at the memory, Josh huffed. "It's the same dream over and over. A hawk, swirling on the air currents, suddenly swoops down and gives me one of its feathers."

Night Hawk nodded thoughtfully.

"It means something," Josh said. "I just don't know what."

"A sacrifice," Night Hawk said. "You must make a sacrifice."

Josh frowned. "Give up something?"

"You are holding on to something that must be set free."

He flapped his hands loosely at his sides. "But what?"

"Something old?" Night Hawk suggested.

Lydia came to his mind. His wife, the life, the family and home she'd created for him.

"Or is it something new?" Night Hawk asked.

Annie. Young and strong, so different from everything he'd known.

Josh looked at his friend and shook his head. "But which is it?"

Night Hawk smiled. "Only you know the answer, my friend."

Josh turned away. He was to give up something. But what should he give up? His past?

Or Annie?

* * *

Weary, Josh strode into the cookhouse and spied Mrs. Royce standing at one of the worktables. "I need something to eat."

Mrs. Royce pinched her lips together. "There's nothing prepared," she spat, and jerked her chin away.

Josh stopped in his tracks. He'd never heard Mrs. Royce speak in that tone, in all the time she'd worked for him.

"Annie's gone," Mrs. Royce informed him, barking the words.

"Gone? To church? To her mother's?"

"*Gone,*" she declared, slamming the lid down on a big pot. "Gone, and not likely to come back."

Stunned, Josh stared at the woman clattering pots and lids together. "What do you mean, she's gone?"

"You'd know the reason better than me, Mr. Ingalls." Mrs. Royce shook a wooden spoon at him. "And you've got company, though I'm sure that's no surprise to you, either. That Mrs. Baird is here, along with your new nanny."

"What the hell are you talking about?"

"Humph!" Mrs. Royce put her nose in the air and stalked away.

Josh headed for the parlor. What the devil was going on? And why, lately, was he the last person to know what was happening in his own home?

He didn't give a damn whether Eleanor Baird was

waiting for him, or some woman claiming to be a nanny. He wanted to talk to Annie.

But first he had to find her. Maybe Eleanor knew where she was.

"Mr. Ingalls," Eleanor gushed, hauling herself off of the settee and meeting him in the doorway to the parlor. "I'm glad you've finally come to your senses."

"Eleanor, I need to find Annie."

"Which is exactly the reason I've come here this morning."

"It is?" Josh glanced past her to the young woman sitting in a chair. "What's going on?"

"After being at your party last night and seeing how those Martin women flaunted themselves here, I knew I must speak to you first thing," Eleanor said.

Josh frowned. "About what?"

She pulled herself up straighter. "It's high time you knew the truth about your children's nanny."

Annie stuffed another chemise into the trunk, sniffling and swiping at her tears. When she'd arrived home at her cousin's house this morning, her mother and both her sisters had tried to talk to her, tried to console her.

But Annie would have none of it. They'd finally fled and left her alone to see to Camille's packing. They knew Annie well enough to give her a wide berth on the rare occasions when her emotions got the best of her.

What could she say to them, anyway? That her heart was broken? That she'd fallen in love with a man she'd sincerely like to throttle within an inch of his life?

"Oh!" Annie dragged her sleeve across her cheeks, wiping away another wave of tears. She pushed her sorrow aside and, as it had so many times this morning, anger took its place.

She was mad at the world. At Josh. At herself.

"Annie?"

Josh's voice vibrated in her ears. She spun and saw him standing in the doorway. Her heart hammered in her chest, pounding its way into her throat.

Josh. How she loved him.

Josh. How she hated him.

He stepped into the room. "Annie, I—"

"Go away!" She turned back to the trunk.

"I need to talk to you."

"Oh, *now* you want to talk?" She flung a handful of pantalets into the trunk. "This morning *I* would have liked to talk to *you,* but I couldn't—because you were *gone!*"

"I shouldn't have left like that."

"No, you shouldn't have."

"I was wrong to do that."

"Yes, you were."

"Annie, I really need to talk with you now."

"Why don't you go back home and talk to your *new* nanny?"

"I'd sent letters to agencies months ago and hadn't heard anything," Josh said. "I didn't know that woman was coming. You know how bad the mail service is.''

Annie glanced back over her shoulder, then hated herself for doing it. The sight of him weakened her. She pulled her anger up again.

''I'm not interested in anything you have to say. I'm leaving with Camille, to take her to school in Virginia.''

''Leaving?''

A lump rose in Annie's throat. She turned away, tears blurring her vision as she tossed clothing into the trunk. ''Yes, leaving to escape the scandal that's surely awaiting me here—thanks to you.''

''What are you talking about?'' He touched her arm, turning her to face him.

''You've ruined my life,'' she told him. ''I care deeply about your children. I don't know how I'll get over them. It suited me fine to wear trousers and simple dresses, until I wore that gown at your party. And I'm probably pregnant.''

His gaze dipped to her belly. ''Do you think so?''

''You've already produced four children! What are the chances I'm not?'' Annie jerked away from him, turning her attention back to her packing. ''Just go away. Leave me alone.''

For several minutes she sensed him standing behind her, felt the warmth he gave off. Then she heard footsteps and a chill passed over her.

A tremor of panic flashed in the pit of her stomach. Had he gone? Had Josh done as she'd asked and left?

Annie turned and saw him standing near the doorway, a harsh, grim look on his face.

"It wasn't supposed to turn out this way," he said.

He sounded bewildered, lost. Annie's anger softened.

"It wasn't supposed to turn out this way," Josh said again, flinging out both hands. "Lydia..."

Oh, God, his wife. The mother of his children. Annie's heart sank into her stomach. Was Josh, as she had always feared, about to tell her he still loved his wife?

"I married Lydia years ago, and that was supposed to be it," Josh said. "I was set. That part of my life was handled. I wasn't supposed to be..."

"Alone?"

Josh shook his head. "Sorry. I wasn't supposed to be sorry."

"Sorry she died?"

He looked at Annie. "Sorry I'd married her."

"Oh, Josh..." Her own anger and hurt forgotten, Annie wanted to run to him, to hold him, but sensed he needed to tell her more.

"I married Lydia even though I didn't love her and knew she didn't love me. But she was what I wanted in a wife—a well-bred woman who could provide me with a proper home. I had what she needed in a husband—money. I thought it would be enough. I really did."

"But it wasn't?" Annie asked.

Josh shook his head. "No. Not nearly enough. I

fought like hell to make myself content with our marriage. It was, after all, just what I'd asked for. And I managed to do just that for a while. But then, it wasn't enough. Not for either of us.

"Then, when I met you, I realized how wrong I had been," Josh continued. "But admitting to myself that I loved you, Annie, was the same as admitting that I'd wasted ten years of my life. Wasted it on a loveless marriage. It was the same as saying I'd been wrong—about everything. Everything, Annie, for the last ten years."

The words seemed to rob Josh of his strength. He slumped down on the bed, quiet for a long time before he looked up at her again.

"I went to see Night Hawk this morning. That's why I left you. He told me I need to give up something—my past or…you."

Annie's heart beat a little faster. She was afraid to hear his decision, but knew she had to. "And what have you decided?"

Josh grinned. "The past, of course. I want you, Annie. If you'll have me."

Warmth spread through Annie, filling her with all the love her heart held for him. But, remembering, she held herself back.

"You may not want me," she said softly, "after you know the truth about my family."

"Oh, yes, this scandal of yours." Josh waved his hand, dismissing her words. "Eleanor Baird came by the house this morning, only too happy to tell me about your sister."

Annie gasped, pushing aside her anger at Eleanor, worrying about Josh's reaction. "And?"

"I don't give a damn what Eleanor or anyone else in the settlement thinks."

"You say that now, but what about in the future?" Annie shook her head. "You won't be happy with everyone talking about me and my family."

Josh rose from the bed. "Is that a reason for us to be apart? Because of what people might say?"

She glanced up at him. "Only you can answer that question. And remember, you'll be answering for your children, as well."

"How's this for my answer—I want you to marry me."

Annie gasped. "You do?"

"Yes." Josh slid his arms around her and pulled her close. "I love you, Annie. I know what that feels like now. I didn't…before. But I don't want to lose it. I don't want to lose you. Will you marry me?"

Annie wanted to throw her arms around his neck and accept his proposal quickly, but couldn't.

"There're a few things you need to know first," she said.

"More secrets?"

"No."

"Good, because I don't like secrets. No more secrets between us."

"Fine," she agreed. "But there are a few things that will have to change. First, I'm not going to shuffle the children off somewhere else all the time.

They'll be with us. We'll be together. A real family.''

Josh nodded. ''I like that idea.''

''And I'm going to pack away all those fancy things in the house so the children will be comfortable there and we won't have to worry about them breaking things.''

''Suits me fine.''

''And…'' Annie's cheeks heated. ''And I'm not going to have a separate bedroom like Lydia did.''

Josh grinned. ''This is quite a burden you're putting on me, having my wife in my bed every night. But I'll manage.''

She looped her arms around his neck. ''Then, yes, I'll marry you.''

Josh leaned down and kissed her, drawing her close against him.

''So you're not going to Virginia with Camille?'' he asked.

''Maybe we could both go with her?''

He thought for a moment. ''Maybe we could.''

''What about the nanny that showed up at your house this morning? What are you going to do about her?''

Josh shrugged. ''We'll find work for her somewhere.''

''Ours might not be the next marriage in the settlement,'' Annie said. ''Mama told me Thomas proposed last night.''

''Well, I'll be damned. Good for them.''

''He's taking Mama back to St. Louis with him.

I'm sure she'll be happier there,'' Annie said. "He's not ashamed of Willa, either. In fact, he's determined to track down the Keller family, and let the two young people make their own decision.''

"I'd say we've plenty of reason to celebrate,'' Josh said. He reached over her head and pushed the door closed. "I'd like to pick up where we left off last night.''

Annie blushed. "Josh, it's broad daylight.''

He grinned and muzzled her neck. "Yes, but it's Sunday morning. Almost Sunday afternoon. Near enough?''

Annie leaned into him. "Near enough.''

* * * * *

*Please turn the page
for an exciting
preview of Judith's
August 2001 book,*

*THE WIDOW'S
LITTLE SECRET.*

Chapter One

Nevada, 1887

It just wasn't right being envious of a dead man. Still, that's how Jared McQuaid felt sitting on the hotel porch, watching the funeral procession roll by.

He glanced down at the *Stanford Gazette* on his lap. The headline announced the untimely death of Del Ingram, and the front page article extolled the man's many virtues.

A knot formed in Jared's stomach. What were the chances? He'd showed up in this town just today and read the obituary of a man he'd grown up with miles and miles from here. A man he hadn't thought of in years.

According to the newspaper, Ingram had died from a fall. Jared had figured that ol' Del was more likely to have been killed by a jealous husband, an irate wife, or a poker player with an eye for cheaters.

Not so, according to the newspaper. Del had made

something of himself here in Stanford. Owner of a restaurant, a solid citizen with a sterling reputation. A life any man would envy.

Jared touched his hand to the U.S. Marshal's badge pinned to his vest beneath his coat. Seemed he and his boyhood friend had taken very different roads when they parted company some fifteen years ago. This wasn't the man Jared remembered. But maybe Del had changed.

Jared sure as hell had.

The rocker creaked as Jared leaned back and watched from beneath the brim of his black Stetson as the funeral procession passed by. Matched sorrels pulled the wagon bearing the coffin, their hoofs stirring up little swirls of dust. Two dozen mourners followed, all dressed in black, their somber faces flushed red from the raw March wind.

Jared glanced west. Charcoal clouds hung over the Sierra Nevadas blocking out what was left of the day's sunlight. He had nothing to do, no place to go, no one to talk to until morning when he would relieve Stanford's sheriff of his two prisoners and head to Carson City. He may as well pay his respects to Del Ingram, even though he'd never especially liked him.

A few people glanced at Jared as he fell into step behind the mourners. One woman eyed the Colt .45 strapped to his hip and the badge on his chest as the wind whipped open his coat. She chanced a look at his face, then turned away wondering, he was sure, who he was and why he was here.

Jared found himself on the receiving end of a hundred such looks nearly every time he came to a town like this. Not that he blamed anyone of course. He'd arrive one day, eat supper alone in some restaurant, sleep in a nameless hotel, then take custody of his prisoner the following morning and disappear.

And those were his good days. Most of the time he was on the trail, sleeping in the saddle, eating jerky and cold beans, hunting down some rabble rouser who'd broken the law.

He was used to both—the life and the looks he got. Jared had been a marshal for nearly ten years now.

At the cemetery on the edge of town, six men unloaded the coffin from the wagon. Del Ingram's final resting place was deep; fresh-turned earth lay beside it.

Reverend Harris stepped to the foot of the grave, yanked his black, wide-brimmed hat over the tufts of his gray hair, and struggled to hold open the fluttering pages of his Bible. The townsfolk gathered in a close knot, straining to hear the reverend's words. Jared moved off to one side, uncomfortable among the mourners.

As was his custom, Jared's gaze moved from face to face sizing up each person assembled there. He was good at it. It had saved his life a time or two.

From all appearances, everyone who was anyone in the town of Stanford was assembled to mourn Del's passing. They all looked prosperous, in dress and in manner. Jared spotted the mayor and his wife.

He'd met the man earlier in the sheriff's office. Sheriff Hickert wasn't present but Jared hadn't expected him to be. He was nursing a nasty leg wound from the shoot-out that had garnered the two prisoners Jared was transporting tomorrow.

The gathering shifted as Reverend Harris reached for the woman standing in front of him. Jared's stomach bottomed out.

"Damn...."

The widow. Del's widow. Jared felt like he'd been sucker-punched in the gut.

He didn't know how Ingram had acquired a prosperous business, a good name, a sterling reputation—and he sure as hell couldn't imagine how he'd found himself such a fine-looking wife.

Even in her mourning dress she looked fit and shapely. She'd draped a black lace scarf over her head but tendrils of her hair escaped in the wind and blew across her pale cheeks. She stood stiff and straight, her full lips pressed tightly together as she gazed past the reverend to some point on the distant horizon.

Jared thought she looked brave, determined not to break down. He wondered if she'd fully accepted the sudden loss of her husband, dead not quite two days now. He'd seen that happen before, where a long time passed before reality finally set in and only then did loved ones fall to pieces.

Who would be there to hold Mrs. Del Ingram when that happened? Jared wondered. He wondered, too, why the thought bothered him so much.

He recalled the newspaper article he'd read and remembered no mention of Ingram having any children. Indeed, no little ones hung on Mrs. Ingram's skirt, sniffling, reaching up to her. Jared found that troubling. The widow was truly alone now, it seemed, without even a child to comfort her.

"Let us pray," Reverend Harris called.

As heads bowed, Jared pulled out the newspaper he'd crammed into his pocket and searched for the widow's name. Matilda. Mattie, the mayor's wife had called her in a quote.

He turned to her again. His breath caught. Mattie Ingram hadn't bowed her head for the prayer. She looked straight at him.

Their gazes met and held. She didn't blink, didn't falter, didn't hesitate, just looked at him long and hard with the biggest, brownest eyes he'd ever seen.

Heat plumed in Jared's belly, spreading outward, weakening his knees and causing his heart to thump harder in his chest.

"Amen," the reverend intoned.

"Amen," the gathering echoed.

Only then did Mattie turn away. Flushed, Jared pushed back his coat to welcome the chilly wind.

He watched her, silently willing her to turn toward him again. But she didn't. Rigid, restrained, Mattie accepted condolences, then headed back to town with the mourners crowded around her.

Standing beside the mound of dirt at Ingram's grave, Jared followed her with his gaze, the bustle under her dark dress swaying, the vision of her deep brown eyes still boring into him. Finally, she disappeared from sight. Jared headed for the closest saloon....

*   *   *   *   *

Harlequin truly does
make any time special. . . .
This year we are celebrating
weddings in style!

A
Walk
Down
the Aisle
WEDDING CELEBRATION

To help us celebrate, we want you to tell us how wearing the Harlequin wedding gown will make your wedding day special. As the grand prize, Harlequin will offer one lucky bride the chance to **"Walk Down the Aisle" in the Harlequin wedding gown!**

There's more...

For her honeymoon, she and her groom will spend five nights at the **Hyatt Regency Maui.** As part of this five-night honeymoon at the hotel renowned for its romantic attractions, the couple will enjoy a candlelit dinner for two in Swan Court, a sunset sail on the hotel's catamaran, and duet spa treatments.

Maui • Molokai • Lanai

To enter, please write, in, 250 words or less, how wearing the Harlequin wedding gown will make your wedding day special. The entry will be judged based on its emotionally compelling nature, its originality and creativity, and its sincerity. This contest is open to Canadian and U.S. residents only and to those who are 18 years of age and older. There is no purchase necessary to enter. Void where prohibited. See further contest rules attached. Please send your entry to:

Walk Down the Aisle Contest

In Canada	In U.S.A.
P.O. Box 637	P.O. Box 9076
Fort Erie, Ontario	3010 Walden Ave.
L2A 5X3	Buffalo, NY 14269-9076

You can also enter by visiting www.eHarlequin.com
Win the Harlequin wedding gown and the vacation of a lifetime!
The deadline for entries is October 1, 2001.

HARLEQUIN®
Makes any time special ®

PHWDACONT1

INDULGE IN A QUIET MOMENT
WITH HARLEQUIN

Get a FREE
Quiet Moments Bath Spa

with just two proofs of purchase from any of our four special collector's editions in May.

Harlequin® is sure to make your time special this Mother's Day with four special collector's editions featuring a short story *PLUS* a complete novel packaged together in one volume!

Collection #1 Intrigue abounds in a collection featuring *New York Times* bestselling author Barbara Delinsky and Kelsey Roberts.

Collection #2 Relationships? Weddings? Children? = *New York Times* bestselling author Debbie Macomber and Tara Taylor Quinn at their best!

Collection #3 Escape to the past with *New York Times* bestselling author Heather Graham and Gayle Wilson.

Collection #4 Go West! With *New York Times* bestselling author Joan Johnston and Vicki Lewis Thompson!

Plus Special Consumer Campaign!

Each of these four collector's editions will feature a "FREE QUIET MOMENTS BATH SPA" offer. See inside book in May for details.

Only from

HARLEQUIN®
Makes any time special ®

Don't miss out! Look for this exciting promotion on sale in May 2001, at your favorite retail outlet.

MONTANA MAVERICKS

Bestselling author

SUSAN MALLERY

WILD WEST WIFE

THE ORIGINAL MONTANA MAVERICKS HISTORICAL NOVEL

**Jesse Kincaid had sworn off love forever.
But when the handsome rancher kidnaps
his enemy's mail-order bride to get revenge,
he ends up falling for his innocent captive!**

RETURN TO WHITEHORN, MONTANA, WITH

WILD WEST WIFE

Available July 2001

**And be sure to pick up
MONTANA MAVERICKS: BIG SKY GROOMS,
three brand-new historical stories about Montana's
most popular family, coming in August 2001.**

HARLEQUIN®

Makes any time special®

Visit us at www.eHarlequin.com

PHWWW

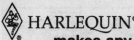